ANCIENT MEMORIES
FUTURE DREAMS

The Crystal Skull Diaries

Solange Arbesú-Sala

Published by Dagaz Press

ISBN: 0615826954
ISBN-13: 978-0615826950
Library of Congress Control Number: 2014933558
Dagaz Press, San Francisco, CA

Cover design by Margarita Camarena

ANCIENT MEMORIES
FUTURE DREAMS

The Crystal Skull Diaries

ACKNOWLEDGMENTS

There are many whom I wish to thank for making this book possible.

Lis Retzmann, my editor and dear friend who painstakingly edited every draft I have written - oftentimes with humor and very much love. I thank you from the bottom of my heart.

Talia Shafir, who flew in from somewhere up above and landed on the page at the very last minute bringing her wonderful gifts of clarity and far-sightedness.

Sheryl Mercure, for her vision - who saw the form this book would take long before I did. Joyce Brown, Suteja Navarro and Christine Wright for the power of their knowledge, wisdom and insights in all things esoteric. Margarita Camarena, for capturing in art what I conveyed in words in the cover of this book. Christiane Arbesu, my sister, whose comments were instrumental and who would never lie to me.

I am indebted to Daphne Rose McCoy, Angela Murphy, Marina Zharkina, Peggy Tahir, Dede Murphy, Wendy McGill, Franco Herrera, and Karen Klein, for their invaluable support. Erik Hansen whose generosity and love welcomed me back to the US when I needed it most.

To my friends and family for all their love and support. A special thank you to the Penzance community that I was blessed to have been a part of for many years. And lastly, to Anna Mitchell-Hedges. I shall always cherish the three years I spent visiting her in Newton Abbott, UK – sharing endless cups of tea and biscuits as we marveled at the magic and the mystery that is the crystal skull. Until we meet again.

CHAPTER ONE

I am the curator of Ethnography at the British Museum, yet I know nothing. I have the qualifications but what does a piece of paper mean? Only that you have studied and passed the required academic curriculum. I thought that having letters after my name would fill the insecurity that seeped through the letters in my own name, Eliot Addison Pierce. But this isn't a story about me – not really, although I play a part. I started as a rook that somehow stumbled his way into the position of king without knowing what chess was really all about. I found myself doing things I would not normally do – like steal a priceless object. That word is rather harsh in these circumstances but steal I did for a while – until I could return that which did not belong to me to its rightful owner. The Book of Runes says that 'in each life there comes at least one moment which if recognized and seized, transforms the course of that life forever.'[1] I recognized the moment but seizing it was something altogether different.

I had just finished giving an evening lecture on Ritual in Mesoamerica and was on my way out, when Nigel, one of the security guards, nudged me.

---

1   Blum, Ralph, The Book of Runes, (New York, NY: St. Martin's Press, 1982), 127

"Look who's over there," he said.

"Who," I said, to be polite. I really just wanted to leave.

Nigel nodded his head towards the left corner of the room. I halfheartedly turned around.

"La Priestess," he said.

My heart skipped a beat although I didn't know who he was referring to at first. And then I saw her. I hadn't seen her in several years. She had long wavy hair the color of chestnuts. Tonight it was pulled back tightly and it was the first time that I could really see her face. It was heart shaped and with her hair up like that she looked much younger than I'm sure she must have been.

She had on a sea green velvet coat, a style reminiscent of another era, and a gold filigree brooch which sparkled with garnets.

"Elegant, isn't she?" Nigel said.

I was startled, forgetting for a moment where I was and who was speaking to me.

"What was it that you called her?" I asked.

"La Priestess," Nigel said. "Suits her, don't you think?"

"But why do you call her that?"

"I don't know. All us guards call her that. She used to come here all the time when the crystal skull was on display. She only stopped when the skull wasn't on show anymore. You must have seen her. Don't you remember?

"I remember," I said.

"She used to stand in front of that skull or sometimes she would sit on one of the benches and stare at it for hours. She always came alone and looked as if she wasn't doing anything other than daydreaming," Nigel said.

"Yes, I used to wonder what she was up to," I said.

"She seems different from the other visitors."

"What?" I said. I hadn't listened properly. All my attention was focused on her.

"You know the type," Nigel continued, "the ones wearing crystals of every description. And there was always a guide or leader of the group of visitors who would have everyone enthralled with stories of the skull's mysterious power."

"To be honest, Nigel, I never really paid attention to those people - just her. I'm intrigued."

"She looks sad." Nigel said.

At that moment she looked up and our eyes met and somehow I found myself walking towards her.

"Hello, I'm Eliot, but I guess you already know that," I said, trying in vain to suppress the cough forcing itself from my throat. Introducing myself on a one-to-one basis has never been one of my strengths.

"Hi, I'm Mia," she said.

"I've seen you here before," I said.

"Yes, I've seen you, too."

"Oh," I said. That comment had taken me by surprise. It never occurred to me that she would have ever paid any attention to me. Maybe she was a thief. Don't they spend years planning their heist?

"You're interested in the crystal skull." I said.

"Yes." She replied.

"Would you like to go out for a cup of tea or coffee? I would really like to hear about it."

"Alright, why not? That would be nice."

Her smile was encouraging, not at all what I had expected. It was the warmth of that smile that hit me, totally catching me unawares.

"American?" I asked.

"Yes."

After what seemed like a very long pause, I tried again. "What is your interest in the skull? I know that people are intrigued by it, by the mystery of its origins, an exact replica of a female Mayan skull carved out of quartz crystal. Well, you've just heard my lecture and I'm sure you know all that anyway."

"I love museums," Mia said, "especially this one. I was so excited about coming here tonight knowing that you were giving a lecture on Ritual in Mesoamerica and that the crystal skull was going to feature in your lecture. I was even hoping that the skull would be exposed, not encased in Plexiglas with no air or sunlight like it was before. And then there's all the pilfering, they call it acquiring ancient and valuable artifacts, but basically we're talking about stealing. Just look around you – half of Egypt is in here."

She was animated, and I couldn't help but feel like she was blaming me for the injustices perpetrated by museums in general.

"Hang on a minute," I said. "One thing at a time".

"Sorry, I didn't mean to go off on you like that."

She glanced at the exit and moved slightly as if to let me know that she wished to leave.

"There is a small café around the corner on Coptic St. Shall we go there?" I had to move fast if I was to stop her from walking off.

That smile again – when we walked into the café I was surprised that the proprietor knew her by name.

"I'm staying on Montague Street. I come in here a lot," she explained.

"So, you're not affiliated with any scientific organization?"

"No."

"Are you writing a thesis of some kind?"

"No, I don't have any of the qualifications that would satisfy you." She said it as if she were challenging me.

"You never did answer my question about the skull."

She took a deep breath but didn't answer immediately, sipping her drink instead. She looked at me then, not in-directly like most people do, but looked right inside. The café seemed to disappear and the space between all things grew larger and enveloped us. She looked at me for a long time and I let her. I knew that I couldn't hide even if I had wanted to. Those few seconds it took me to relax into it really did feel like an eternity. At first unpleasant, but there is something exhilarating about finally allowing someone to see who you are, glimpsing own image as it reflects back through them. I knew that what I was about to hear would change my perception of what I believed the world to be, although I couldn't fully grasp its meaning at the time.

"Do you really want to hear this? It's not something I share very often."

"Uh-huh," I responded, sounding more like Cro-Magnon man. If I was going to let myself be seen, she sure was going to as well, I thought.

"Okay," she said, leaning forward on the table. I imitated her, wanting in on the secret.

"Your lecture scratched the surface of what the skull is about. You give the empirical evidence and, of course, it's important to do that. People need to get just how special the skull is and that we don't have the technology to carve it. It was carved against the grain of the crystal which, for all intents and purposes, should have made it shatter. But there is so much more. Scientists can't tap into its power because they're going about it the wrong way."

I was intrigued and Mia continued.

"When I came here tonight, I was so upset. Unfortunately, you happened to be the one who received the brunt of it. So I am truly sorry about that. What is upsetting me so much is this attitude that whoever is in power, can just take - take what doesn't belong to them - show it off, acquire it for personal gain and profit. Basically, everything that's wrong with the world seemed to be screaming at me through the artifacts laid out so perfectly by your so-called specialists. Sacred objects locked up, unused and rendered impotent."

"But there's so much that is positive about museums. The richness of so many cultures gathered in one building, preserved, protected and passed down from generation to generation."

"Yes, and now I understand something that I didn't before. There are certain artifacts, power objects, if you like, that are designed specifically as tools for transformation in consciousness. Are you with me so far?"

"I think so."

"Okay. So, although they did not know it, museums have been able to protect these sacred objects until such time that they can be of use. The crystal skull is such an object. It is here, lying dormant waiting for the right person or people to come along to access the knowledge and to free up the energy and power it contains. I believe that there will come a time when curators will be of an entirely different kind. They will understand how to work with these ancient artifacts, how to access the knowledge and then teach the information. The curators then will be more like shamans, healers and visionaries."

"Curators as shamans? Well, I'm intrigued. But what does the skull have to do with you?"

"Let's just say I know how to work with it," she said.

"Are you saying that you yourself are a shaman?"

"No, not in the traditional sense, but something like that."

The mind is a funny thing. You are given a truth and you are in the moment with it. Truth carries a certainty that can propel you forward - sometimes at lightning speed, other times meekly. But somewhere along the way, if your mind is not in harmony with your spirit, truth can seem to get lost again in the labyrinth of doubt. Was she telling the truth?

Her intense dark eyes spoke for her as she sat there looking at me pondering in my doubt. She was not unkind but rather sympathetic. I wanted to say, "I think you're mistaken; it is I that should be feeling sorry for you. I know my place in this world. Clearly, you do not." But I was too polite. And yet, I felt inadequate.

"I hope you didn't take offense to what I said about the curators of the future and about museums."

Mia's words brought me back into the conversation.

"No, not at all," I lied.

"It's just that I don't often get a chance to talk to someone like you, you know, as an expert on ancient traditions. You have an important job at the museum - you are well respected. It's people like you that can affect change."

"Well, thank you," I replied. Hearing her give me some credence made me feel better.

She nodded and I knew that she wanted to leave.

We said goodbye and stepped out into the brisk London air and I walked her back to her hotel. We walked in silence and I was surprised at how comfortable that felt. I half expected her to place her arm around mine but of course she didn't.

"Good night and thank you again," she said and we parted.

I stood there staring at the black door long after she had gone inside. Turning my back, I clearly and distinctly heard a voice.

"This is only the beginning," it said.

☙

I walked all the way home. It took well over an hour and I was cold but I didn't care. My mind was reeling. I went home, had a glass of water and went to bed. It was 3:30 in the morning when I woke up and put pen to paper, transcribing what I had dreamt. I dreamt of the skull hovering in front of me and then it somehow was on my face. It was warm and blended in with my features. I then saw myself reading from a great big book and, at the same time, found myself following along like you do when at a recital....

The story has already been told — an old story buried deep within the recesses of your memory. The only way forward is to remember the past. The only way forward is to be in the present, linked up like a fine gold chain with the richness of the past pushing you forward, to where the future lies. Deep within us, we also know what lies ahead, for that too is another link in the chain. Wear your memories like a bracelet so that if you gaze down to look at it or to softly touch it, you can remember. And then the memories surface like the smell of something wonderful and long forgotten. The scent wafts by under your nose, teasingly, as if to say, 'Smell me, go on, do you remember?' And you take a deep breath — no hesitations — you fill your lungs deeply, as much as you can take in so that every part of you opens up and the memories come flooding back in sweetness and in fullness. In that moment, there is no longing because you are already there.

They say that the eyes are the windows to the soul. Looking through the eyes of the skull is another doorway, a gateway into one's past and future and a way to make sense of the present. Wear the skull like a mask, so that you become one and look through its eyes. That missing link that really isn't missing but rather misplaced. Where do you want to go? What do you need to see? Ask in a whisper for then the secrets that lay buried can gently flow up to the surface of your consciousness — awakening to a new time and place.

At this moment, we speak as one to show you that we are here to communicate knowledge through a system of energy and that you can access this regardless of whether we have been 'found' or not. We can be likened to the thoughts of the Gods made manifest in crystalline form.

To work with us is to work with power — power in the true sense of the word, enabling you to be all that you are. It is important to understand how we work energetically because this is the way to access us. We are translating and transmitting our energy into the written word — the language evokes a response or a memory from deep within you so that when you sit quietly and call us to you, we will be familiar.

We come in the form of skulls to show you that we are like you and you like us. The knowledge that we carry is your knowledge — your history, your wisdom and your truth. The past informs who you were, the present informs who you are and the future informs what you will become. But what you will become you already are. It is a paradox. Imagine then that you can see everything there is to see in an instant. You are sitting somewhere up above the clouds looking down on earth. You are there for a long time looking down with your hand resting on your chin, with one foot dangling, like the man on the moon. All you need do is observe the scene below and look for the hidden treasures.

What is your memory? What is your story? Your story is the same as ours although the names, places and events may differ but the resonance of the experience is similar because we come from the same place.

෴

I wrote this quickly and succinctly - as a scribe might very well have done. I half imagined myself in a different time with quill and ink transcribing the knowledge of an age whose wisdom would only come to light thousands of years in the future. And I was excited because you see; I have always wanted to be a writer. 'Here's a good start to a story,' I thought.

And what makes you think you wrote this? Here was another voice speaking to me in my head - twice in one night.

"It's my handwriting. Of course I wrote it." I replied back out loud as if my voice would give me the confidence and the justification I was seeking. I heard laughter then, a deep throaty laugh - not the kind that's scary as you would think when you hear disembodied laughter, but more the kind that found what I had just said so funny, so witty. It confused me. Nevertheless, my knees were shaking.

I couldn't sleep after that. I knew that Mia was a part of this somehow and that she would have answers. It never occurred to me to ask her for her mobile number - I didn't even know her surname. I really wasn't thinking at all that night but at least I knew where she was staying.

⚜

"I'm sorry, Sir," the girl behind the reception said. "But Mia's left. She's gone down to Penzance."

"Penzance?"

"Yes, Sir, in Cornwall."

"Yes, I know where Penzance is, but could you tell me when she left and what she's doing down there?"

"I don't know, Sir."

At that moment, the owner arrived.

"Hello, I'm Mrs. Higgins. And you are…?"

"Eliot, Eliot Pierce."

"I thought so" she said, "Mia left you a note."

"Julia, why didn't you ask this gentleman for his name?" She reprimanded the girl. "I told you Mia was expecting him."

I made my polite goodbyes and found myself standing outside that black front door again, tearing open the note.

Inside was her business card. All it had was her name, Mia Delacroix, and both American and English telephone numbers. When I turned it over, she had written a message, 'In case you need to get hold of me,' it read.

The last time I was in Cornwall, my friend Stephen had been researching divination practices from around the world and wanted to interview some of the locals in various parts known for their Celtic 'abilities', so I tagged along. In Penzance, we heard about this woman named Margaret Poxa, who was well respected. Margaret was a clairvoyant and gave psychic readings. She had the ability to look inside of you, see aspects of yourself from other lifetimes and how they related to your present, even future self. She could communicate not only with her 'guides' but with yours as well. They came to her so that they could assist in your personal development. She was like a counselor, therapist and spiritual healer all rolled into one. I decided to have a 'reading' with her to see what this was all about.

⚜

She told me that I had been a very powerful Romanian gypsy leader who not only was a businessman but was also responsible for keeping alive the spiritual and mystical traditions of the tribe – much like a shaman. She also said that I had a female lover in every port! But that part really wasn't important - what was important was that I carried this universal message of always wanting to help my people out of division and greed – to turn everybody and everything around in order to make things right. I remember now word for word what she had said about a woman:

"There will come a time where all of your structures will be challenged and with that will come a rebirth. A woman with long dark hair, slightly older, and who may seem strange to you at first will be a part of this transformation. She will assist you in awakening your cellular memory. You will have incredible awareness. People are not going to recognize you. I see a lot of your shyness - the way your expression gets squashed, clearing up. And that's because when you work in the spiritual realms, you have to work on releasing a lot of things that no longer serve you. You have to make room for the energy to come in. If you don't make room for it, the energy comes in, goes through and has no place to stay."

I hadn't thought about that reading since it happened. It did resonate with me then but I guess I was too focused on the part about a "female lover in every port", which is so unlike me now, that I really didn't give much thought to the rest of it. As for past lives, well, I hadn't thought about that either but a dark-haired woman had come into my life and left a trail of sorts. And there I was scrambling in search of something that I didn't quite know what to make of.

CHAPTER TWO

The best kind of changes I believed, were the gradual ones, like slow water on rock to smooth out life's hard edges. That way you'd have the time to investigate, get right in there and take a look at what is transpiring moment by moment. The thought of change cracking open and tumbling out without warning only appealed to me in the study of civilizations long gone like researching the fall of Pompeii. And excitement meant finding out about someone else's discovery or theory. So when change appeared in my life, I didn't have the time to take a look at how and where it was leading me. My old default mechanisms stalled and sputtered, and I was left, instead, hanging on to change's tail, hoping the ride would at least be amenable. It wasn't easy then to make that phone call, yet something was propelling me forward.

"Ur, hello Mia, this is Eliot Pierce – we met at the museum."

"Eliot, hang on a minute, let me get off the other line."

Those precious few seconds gave me the chance to get hold of myself.

"Hi, Eliot, how are you?"

"Well, thanks, and you?"

"Fine."

"I don't really know what to make of all this, but after I saw you, I had this strange experience. I'm not really sure what to call it - but it has to do with the crystal skull."

"I'm not surprised."

"Is that why you left your number?"

"Look, before we get into that, can I ask how long you'll be in Cornwall? I'd love to talk to you in person, if that's okay."

"I'll be here for a while. Why don't you come down? It doesn't take all that long to get here, maybe six hours at most," Mia said.

"Not that long? Well, you definitely must be American in thinking that six hours isn't a long drive," I said, laughing.

'But all right, yes, I think I will drive down. I'll stay at the Blue Diamond Inn. I've only ever been there a couple of times but I like their accommodations. I'll give 'em a ring."

"Great, that's a nice place," Mia said. "Just let me know when you'd like to meet up. I live on Morrab Place. It's only a short walk from the Blue Diamond and you can drop by."

"Okay then, I'll get on the case and call you when I arrive."

I packed a few things into a small suitcase along with a bottle of the finest single malt whisky as well as the pages I had written. I had so much work going on at the museum that I sort of lumped the experience of that night with my work and didn't equate it with anything personal. I think it was because of this that I hadn't really thought about what I was getting into and how it would affect my personal life.

But my body had a mind of its own. There was a tension of sorts building and my body ached as if I'd had a long workout.

The good thing though was that the drive was uneventful and exactly six hours later, I arrived. It was late already and I wouldn't have called Mia at that hour but as fate would have it, she rang me.

"How's the long distance traveler?" she said

"A little weary but in one piece," I said, half joking.

"Have you eaten?"

"Nope, I was thinking of stopping soon to see what I could find."

"Nothing decent is open this time of night. I've got some homemade soup, so why not drop by?"

"That sounds perfect. I'll be there in a minute. Where exactly are you though?"

There wasn't time to think about the familiarity with which we addressed each other I thought, as I walked the few blocks to her house. All I knew was that I liked what was happening.

It was two o'clock in the morning when I made my way back to the hotel. When I awoke, I knew more than I have ever known before. I felt more than I have ever felt before and I reveled in it. The world was opening up to me, it seemed.

I guess I'm getting ahead of myself though and I would, for the sake of continuity, like to follow the events in the order in which they occurred. But when your life shifts from the ordinary to the extraordinary, events take on an abstract pattern rather than a linear one. Your senses sharpen and you start to see and hear with your feelings. And somewhere between the logical and the abstract, new patterns emerge – where you are at the center – orchestrating a symphony as both conductor and magician of your own destiny. You do, after all, use the same wand.

✺

I found myself inside a Georgian townhouse. It was only a stone's throw from the sub-tropical Morrab Gardens and had a grandeur that matched the neighboring Georgians which were twice its size. There was a roaring fire in the living room and a few candles lit on several small tables. I felt comfortable stepping into this atmosphere and I was filled with a warmth that had nothing to do with the fire. I ate in the kitchen with Mia – an old country kitchen with a big shiny red Aga cooker. The lentil soup was delicious and the Irish Soda bread, the perfect accompaniment.

"Did you make the bread as well?" I asked.

"No, Marks and Spencer's did. I went up to Truro earlier to get some things. But that oven really deserves to be used - with a color like that.

"Yes, I think you're right. It really is the business." I ate the rest of the soup in silence and Mia, with her arms crossed on the table, watched me.

When I had finished and the tea was brewing, I got up and brought my briefcase in the kitchen and produced the pages I had written the night before.

"Please read this," I said, handing her the pages. What more could I say? The pages would speak for themselves.

"Eliot, all I can think of to say is, wow!"

'That's not all though. I heard a voice inside my own head but I knew it wasn't me."

"What did it say?"

"Well, basically, that I hadn't written this. You see, I kind of was thinking about writing a story around it. It was just an idea I had for a novel."

"A novel?"

"Yes." I suddenly felt embarrassed. It wasn't hard for her to pick that up since my face was turning the color of the stove.

"I guess I should start at the beginning. I woke up in the middle of the night. I don't usually dream but this dream was so vivid. I saw myself standing in front of this book. It was a huge book with gold leaf edges that rested on a marble podium. I was reading from it but at the same time felt as if I was being read to. I remember glancing up for a second, the way you do when there's a natural pause when someone is speaking or reading out loud. And I looked up and saw that I was in a place that was like a mansion with arched doorways but what caught my eye was the floor."

"Black and white checkered tiles," we both said, in unison.

"How did you know that?"

"Shall we go into the living room?" She motioned for us to go into the room and spoke softly, "I don't really know where to begin."

I made myself comfortable on the sofa and she sat cross-legged in a big armchair that seemed to envelope her.

She sat quietly for a while and seemed to think about what to say. I couldn't wait any longer and so I started the conversation.

"Well, what do you make of it?" My words sounded slightly forced to me, although I didn't mean them to be. I guess I was anxious.

"Have you heard of channeling?" Mia asked me.

"Channeling? Isn't that like a clairvoyant allowing for a dead spirit to talk through them?"

"Sort of… there are many ways to communicate with the unseen, shall we say. Channeling isn't just about communicating with disembodied spirits, it's also about being able to tap into the energy of an object to receive the impressions that have been left there. Psychometry is a term often used for this."

"I'm not sure I'm following." I leaned forward, frustrated that I couldn't keep up with her.

"Okay, it's like what I was trying to explain when we met. Everything in the universe is alive, with energy. What we think of as objects can also communicate. And the crystal skull, being made out of quartz, is a natural transmitter and conduit, the perfect material to store information whether it's of an intellectual, spiritual or emotional nature."

She uncrossed her legs, leaned forward and smiled. I thought she had smiled at my forehead which had folded itself into a frustrated frown. I tried to relax my face and she smiled again.

"Think of the skull as a highly advanced computer that can store knowledge in all its forms. And the beauty is that it can't be misinterpreted or lost in translation, as the message is the same in any language. The information is encoded in such a way that only the truth can be revealed. So it wasn't by accident that those that made the skull, known as the guardians, created it out of quartz.

'So how do you think the messages were encoded? I asked, leaning back in my seat again. I could understand 'computer'.

She took a sip of her tea and settled back in her chair crossing her legs and sitting like a yogi.

"It's hard for me to explain. Imagine if all of a sudden there were massive earth changes and we were back in the dark ages. Would you be able to reinvent the technology that we now have? I certainly couldn't. It's kind of like that for me. What I do know, though, is that the knowledge was encoded using sound and light, and the crystal was formed in the shape of a skull. Each group of guardians had their own particular vibration and knowledge to be encoded. That's why there are different skulls made out of amethyst, rose quartz and smoky quartz to name a few. They all have their own particular vibration and spiritual information to convey.

I was fascinated and nodded to let Mia know that I wished for her to continue.

"It's not possible for one person to access all the information but many will receive what they need most or wish to impart. So, for those with a scientific/medical background, for instance, they'll be able to tap into that particular frequency and access the information they need. Others with more of a technological background, will be able to access information suited to their expertise – different vibrations for different gifts and strengths. But the only way to obtain any information at all is to be in alignment with your own mind, body and spirit," Mia said.

"And what about people like you, Mia? What category do you fall under?"

"I guess you could say I tap into the spiritual knowledge that it contains," she said.

"But surely not just anyone can access this knowledge. I've been around the skull and nothing like this has happened to me before, or to anyone that I work with at the museum, at least not that I know of. So why now? Why would the skull want to communicate with me? And why a skull? Why not just a plain crystal ball or a wand, something less imposing, shall we say?"

Mia smiled, knowing that I was trying to be tactful about the imposing part. Nevertheless, there was something else behind that smile, a gentleness, as if she were looking at an innocent. I felt she knew things about me that I didn't and it was somewhat unsettling.

"As you, yourself wrote, Eliot, it is shaped like a skull and contained within it is the knowledge of humankind. And, as you well know, you can't carbon date crystal so no one knows how old the skull is. A symbol, I think, of our immortality.

I was firing questions and the responses were flying right back at me.

"Eliot, you have to be aligned with the energy of the crystal in order for the skull to communicate with you. Clearly something has been building within you for a while. When you have time, think about it and ask yourself, what has changed? Why would your life take on such a turn? Sometimes it takes years before we get the answer so just allow for things to unfold."

She wasn't giving me all the answers then, not what I had expected at all. I was confused, intrigued and slightly agitated all at the same time. But Mia wasn't patronizing. She challenged me and I liked that. I was being challenged in a way that I had never been before. I definitely had to remove the conditioning amassed over the years of how things ought to be in my world. I found I was beginning to unlock a part of myself that I didn't even know existed.

"But you also act as a conduit for others to experience this knowledge, don't you? Like what some would call a medium," I said. "That's why I had that experience, or part of the reason."

She blushed. Perhaps it was because she wasn't used to being the one who is seen and I caught her off guard. It was the first time I saw her vulnerability. I guess I thought that if you were 'connected' to higher spiritual forces then you were somehow immune to the inadequacies of an earthly existence. But of course that is not the case.

"Please don't take this the wrong way," she said, "but I've learnt to keep silent, like not casting your pearls sort of thing. It's that I didn't want to come across as some airy-fairy person. Not that there's anything wrong with that – it's just not who I am."

I nodded, not really knowing what to say, so she continued.

"I wanted you to take me seriously and if you couldn't do that, then our paths wouldn't have crossed again until you could be open to me, to who I am – and what I am."

A silence filled the room and it was palpable. I knew that she spoke the truth, although I didn't know exactly what she meant. There are so many levels of understanding. You think that you 'get it' but in hindsight, you realize that there are layers of meaning and you, in fact, have only scratched the surface. I felt as if I had been split in two. The logical side was the Eliot I knew so well and then there was the abstract Eliot, who understood, although not with his mind. And the magician in the middle? Well, he hadn't quite emerged yet.

✿

"I guess I'll start when I first went to the museum," Mia said. "I was on my way to Cornwall to see the house that I had inherited from my aunt, my dad's sister. She was 16 years older than my dad, a bit of a recluse, a highly intelligent eccentric French woman who chose Penzance as her home. She was an artist, stained glass and abstract stuff. Anyway, I was feeling guilty and sad that I hadn't spent any time with her in a very long while. I was burned out from all the years of caring for my mother before she died and I just hadn't gotten round to visiting. And now it was too late. When you are the last of your family, it brings up a lot of stuff. I felt like my very foundation was shaken – not knowing who I was, where I was headed or the purpose in any of it. I was an orphan and I related to the world in that way, as if I were separate from everyone and everything, observing it all but never a part of any one thing. I had put all the goals most people want to achieve into one bucket and that bucket had nothing whatsoever to do with me. Regrets and feeling excluded got all mixed up. I was in grief and something was fundamentally missing and I was in search of it."

She stopped for a minute, sipping her tea which must have been cold by now. It's funny how pausing can bring about a sense of harmony. It gives you time to reflect on what's just been said and draws you further into the story, like a seduction.

"I love museums," she continued. "I didn't know anyone in London so I booked a room in one of the hotels on Montague Street, just opposite the British Museum. I wanted to be able to take in what it had to offer a little bit at a time, go there at whatever time I felt like. I was planning on staying for a few days. It felt like I had all the time in the world to do what I wanted, when I wanted.

"As soon as I entered the room in which the skull was kept, I knew something was happening to me. And as I drew closer, the feeling only got stronger. My stomach started doing somersaults and I could feel myself expanding. I had never seen the skull before, never even heard about it. But there it was and so familiar to me. It was like a bittersweet memory that I couldn't quite connect with.

Hello, old friend, it said.

"I turned around just to make sure that it wasn't someone addressing me but deep inside, I knew what was happening. This was the moment I'd been waiting for.

Hello, I said back. I just didn't think that you would be locked up. We were speaking to each other telepathically, of course. I could hear it so clearly. And it knew what I was feeling. I was so sad to see that it was encased without sunlight, with no air for so many years and that I couldn't touch it. I couldn't hold what I knew so well in my hands. I wanted to reach out in the way you do when you want to pat a child in endearment. The skull made me feel that way and said:

I have been here for quite some time but in crystal time, it really isn't all that long. Don't focus on the negative. There is so much that is positive. Here I am, here you are, the richness of so many cultures gathered in one building. In here, you can literally time travel. In your hurry to find me, you were not aware, did not see just how many bowed down to you in welcome. You have been well received. Know that in this museum there is so much knowledge for you to tap into. Stand here for a moment then, and allow for your heart and mind to open, to receive."

"It felt as if I were being unzipped and exposed, dissected and picked clean," Mia continued. "All the things that needed to be removed from my spirit body were removed and I could feel energy running through me. Although I couldn't see anything, I instinctively knew that the skull was transmitting a lot of information for me to access later.

Like a computer, it felt as if I were downloading information directly from the skull and it was happening so fast. All I had to do was stand there and allow for this process to run its course. It was a strange sensation, happening simultaneously on many levels – physical, mental, emotional and spiritual. I wasn't afraid; in fact, there was no emotion to speak of. I stood there still and cool. And then it was over. I was put back together again - zipped back up. I was so surprised when I realized that a whole hour had gone by. The skull was beaming at me but there was no more conversation. I knew it was time to leave. And so I did."

"I guess it's my turn to be speechless," I said. The story that was emerging captivated me. Nothing out of the ordinary had ever happened to me up until a few days ago and I knew that the more Mia talked, the more understanding I would have about my own experience with the skull that night.

"And then what happened?" I asked.

I wanted to grab everything, take it all in and think about it all later, as she had done with the skull. I found myself sitting opposite an extraordinary person and despite the fact it was now well past midnight, I felt wide awake.

"I think it's time for coffee," Mia said, yawning and stretching her arms. And I want something sweet to eat too. I can whip up something pretty quickly, like apple crumble with custard or ice cream. Your choice. I have a feeling we're going to be up for quite some time and I need to ground myself with food and coffee," she said, smiling.

And so the conversation was put on hold. I couldn't have cared less about eating. All I wanted was to stay in the living room with the fire and the atmosphere. I guess I was afraid that the moment would be lost and I would lose sight of this feeling. I feared that Mia would pull back somehow. But despite my insecurity, I soon began to realize that you can't push the mysteries to reveal themselves to you. There is a natural flow, always in its own rhythm. What had been shared thus far was important and deserved to be ingested without one's psyche distended beyond recognition. I helped peel and core the apples with the ordinary and the extraordinary blending in just the right measure.

CHAPTER THREE

We had spent quite some time in the kitchen, just chatting. I couldn't even tell you about what. I guess it wasn't important but what I do remember was how it felt - a mixture of awe and ease. It was as if I had known this woman my whole life so it was perfectly natural that I would be in her kitchen gone midnight, peeling and coring apples. But then every once in a while I would catch myself because I really didn't know Mia, this woman who fascinated me and was quite unlike anyone I had met before. We had left all of the mystical stuff in the living room, and the kitchen felt to me like neutral ground – a place to be 'normal.' It was unspoken, but I think we both felt that way. So, when we headed back into the living room with our second cup of coffee, Mia picked up right where she had left off.

"When I got to Penzance I phoned this woman who gives psychic readings. She used to be a friend of my aunt's," Mia said.

"I had met Margaret many years before and she had given me a reading. She told me about a past life of mine, and it all made sense to me because she would say things and I knew what she was going to say just before she said them. It was as if my memory opened up, like when you've been asleep, and you know that you've been dreaming but

29

you just can't remember the dream – it's just out there somewhere, and you're trying to catch it because it's so elusive. Then something someone says triggers the memory, and there it is in front of you. That's what it felt like to me. I knew by the end of the reading that I wanted to see more of this woman – that I wanted her to be my teacher. She explained to me so many things about myself that I had always known but kept silent. She was so self-assured, funny and kind."

"You must be talking about Margaret Poxa," I said.

"Why, yes. Do you know her?"

"Sort of, I had a reading with her as well. I only met her the one time."

"Really? I am intrigued," she said laughing. "I'm so glad that you got to meet Margaret. Isn't she wonderful?"

"Yes, I liked her - not at all what I was expecting. I pictured this older woman sort of like a gypsy. Stereotypical, I know, but I just didn't think that she would be so vibrant and charismatic."

"I know! She's in her seventies, and she makes me feel old with her boundless energy. The glass is always half full when you're with Margaret."

"So, did your reading with Margaret make sense to you?" Mia asked, getting back to the more serious side of the conversation.

"Yes, it did. I'll tell you about it another time. Your story sounds a lot more fascinating than mine, believe me. Please, carry on," I said.

"Okay, but I really do want to hear about it."

"Okay," I said, nodding.

And so Mia continued.

"I went down to Lamorna to see Margaret. I needed some guidance and some answers that I knew she could help me with. When I finished recounting what happened in the museum, Margaret suggested we do a past life regression.

She paused for a moment and looked at me as if to give me an opportunity to ask what that meant.

"I've heard of it, but I don't know what it entails," I said.

"It's like going on a journey – into a deep place of relaxation and meditation, a trance, if you will. From that place, you would be guided to explore, to tune into the lifetimes that have a special resonance or connection to the one you are living now. I wanted some information about my connection with the skull."

Her hair came undone at that moment, tumbling down in soft curls. She twisted it deftly round her fingers and pinned it back up with the hair slide that had fallen to the floor. It was over in a manner of seconds but I captured the image, like in still frames – the loose hair around her shoulders, her pinning it back up, and then strands of hair that would not be contained but rather seemed to be assigned the task of framing and enhancing her face. She looked up as if she were expecting me to continue the conversation, but all I could see was one of Rossetti's paintings come to life.

"Eliot?" She should have added, "*Are you listening?*" but she didn't have to; she knew I had gotten lost somewhere.

I stared at her tongue tied. She looked at me as though unaware of the effect she was having on me.

"Er, sorry," I mumbled. "What were you saying?"

"Have I worn you out?" she said. It's late, and I know that sometimes I can get carried away and lose track of time." She seemed a bit embarrassed.

"Oh, no, not at all," I'm fine, really. Please, this is all so fascinating for me. I really do want to hear more."

I could have kicked myself. I didn't want the evening to end. I wanted, or rather, I needed to know more about her, and about her experiences with the skull. Something was building, and I knew that the time for me to leave wasn't quite just yet.

"I was just telling you of my wanting more information about my connection with the skull," Mia said.

"Of course, sorry. What was it like, the regression?"

And so Mia began recounting her experience. She said that Margaret's voice was deep and powerful, and that it didn't take long for her to feel completely comfortable and at ease. What I experienced though was Mia's voice, deep and powerful, with an intonation that seemed to take me into the Dreamtime, the place where she had once been.

"I was lying on a couch and I remember holding on to this blanket as if it would protect me somehow and give me comfort. It's not that I was afraid – more like apprehensive. This time felt different because it wasn't unexpected, like my first encounter. This was something I had planned, and I was doing my best not to have any expectations.

"Remember, you are only an observer, Margaret had said to me. But it didn't feel that way at all. I felt light-headed, moving in time and space, and then I knew that I had 'landed' somewhere. It was like a place suspended somewhere in space and time because it wasn't like I could see anything. All I could feel was emotion – a lot of it. I'm holding on to my stomach, sort of like I'm trying to keep myself together. I'm scrunched up on the sofa looking as if I have a bad stomach ache but it wasn't physical pain. It was just that there was so much energy concentrated in that one place, I didn't know what to do with myself."

She paused, and we both took a deep breath in anticipation of what was to come.

'Can you see the skull,' Margaret had asked me. The moment she said that, there it was hovering in front of me. I could tell that it was trying to communicate with me but the more I looked at the skull, the more emotional I became. I felt as if I would implode with the intensity of it all. And then I started sobbing those great loud hacking sobs; what I was experiencing was more pain than one human could possibly experience in a lifetime. It wasn't physical pain even though my body did feel very strange. My stomach was tied in knots."

"And then what happened?" I asked. We both had our hands wrapped around our stomachs. I leaned forward to get as close to the experience as possible.

She got up and stretched her legs. She had been sitting yoga style for quite some time. But I could tell that she was also reliving some of the experience and indeed, so was I. My heart actually ached and I was overcome with sadness.

"I need some water, would you like some too?" Mia asked.

"Sure, thanks." I spoke loudly because she had already left the room.

I took my glasses off and sat there with my hands resting at my temples massaging the sides of my head in an attempt to make sense of it all. She came up to me to hand me a glass of water, but I hadn't heard her come in. Startled, I jumped out of my seat which made Mia jump as well spilling some of the water onto my trousers.

"Oh, I'm so sorry, Eliot. I'll go and get a towel."

"I'm okay, really. It's only a little water," I said, putting my glasses back on.

But she had already left the room. It may have felt awkward for Mia soaking me like that, but to be honest, I was grateful for the splash of cold water and the distraction it brought. It was hot in that living room. The fire had died down but it seemed a lot warmer than when I had arrived hours before. This little incident seemed to shift the tension that had been building. Mia recovered her composure quickly enough, sat back in the armchair, crossed her legs once again and continued with her story.

"Margaret could see that I was in distress and that I needed to move through it. The moment she suggested that was the moment I no longer felt sorrow. It just instantly disappeared."

"Why was that, exactly?" I asked.

"Because Margaret was guiding me. I was taking direction from her. I felt completely safe like she is a container enabling me to journey through the Dreamtime. She was like the cord that grounded me to this place and time."

"That's fascinating. So you really need to trust the person that you are doing this with," I said, making sense of it all.

"Absolutely, and not only that, the person has to know what they're doing. That experience opened something up inside of me. If you're not ready to deal with that level of intensity, then it could be potentially damaging. You have to be ready."

"I can see that. But how do you know when you're ready and why were you in so much pain? What could possibly bring about that level of emotion?" I asked.

She sat quietly then - pensive. I did not dare interrupt.

"Let's start with your second question. The feeling was like the pain of an entire planet, of a civilization lost, gone in what seemed to me like seconds. That's where I was, and that's what I felt. What was strange was that my unconscious self knew what was happening, knew what the skull meant to me and what I have commissioned myself to do. It's like an instantaneous knowing of everything there is to know. The paradox, though, is that my conscious self was trying to make sense of what was happening – you know, that innocent, naïve other part that has simply forgotten the intricacies of life beyond everyday reality."

I didn't say anything to that - how could I? I didn't know anything about another reality. Instead, I asked about what I could relate to, the feeling that Mia had described happening in her solar plexus.

"Mia, why was it that you felt so much tension in your solar plexus?"

"That's the feeling place, a powerful energy center," she said. "That's the spot to open up to receive. It's not a matter of necessarily seeing things with your eyes or hearing with your ears. What's happening is that energy center, or chakra, if you like, is opening to receive information."

I looked at her, puzzled. I was trying to keep up but this was all so new to me.

"Let me put it another way," she said.

"Think about being in school, and learning something new – something quite challenging – and you just can't wrap your head around it. Doesn't it sometimes feel like your head is expanding trying to take in the information? And then it starts to ache because there's just so much information coming at you from all directions? Well, the head is another energy center too, another chakra. It's just that with your solar plexus, you are processing information differently. Not all information is processed through the mind. The regression and being introduced to the skull was all so new to me, and challenging. My body was receiving and processing the information, hence the physical sensations of my stomach tied up in knots."

"I think my brain needs to expand some more for me to get all of this but I don't have a headache yet," I said, smiling.

"So please continue with the regression. What happened after Margaret directed you to move beyond your emotions?"

"I could see the skull hovering in front of me although my eyes were closed. Then Margaret told me to ask the skull if I was one of its guardians."

She took a deep breath, and I waited for what seemed a very long time.

"So I asked the skull silently and it spoke back. *What do you think, Mia?*, it said. And in that moment, the memory of what home was, and is, came surfacing back to me with a bittersweet longing – a longing for that place where I was understood and recognized as part of something much greater than myself. That place where there is no such thing as separation, loneliness or fear. I knew that the skull was a part of that wholeness, and that I was one of its guardians. It was clear that I'd chosen to let go of that fact and blocked it out for years and years. The regression and my visit to the museum was my way of seeking to reclaim my connection."

For a few moments, Mia and I sat quietly in the silence, and I respectfully waited for the right moment to ask my next question. She was sharing something with me very dear to her, and I wanted to honor that. Mia had a far-away look on her face, but she turned to look at me then letting me know that she was ready for my next question.

"Why would you want to do that? Why would you walk away from something so powerful when the skull is part of your knowledge?"

"These things are complicated and to be honest, I think it will take me a long time to figure it all out. What I can tell you is that I blocked out a lot of memories because it was so painful to watch those who wanted to use the power of the skulls for ill, to manipulate and destroy. I just didn't want to be a part of it anymore, and I blocked it out. So effectively, it seems that I forgot who I was and I struggled to find my way back, not knowing what it was that I was in search of. You see, when you close a door, you end up shutting out not only the bad things but all of the good as well. When you're in such a dark place, you don't think of that."

Mia paused for a moment and leaned towards me.

"So it wasn't an accident that I ended up in the Americas section of the British Museum. The skull was calling to me, and I heard it with my heart. It was time to become familiar once again. In accepting the knowledge, I knew I would also have to accept the responsibility that goes with it. I was finally ready."

I could tell that Mia was tired and needed to rest.

"It's a lot to take in, Mia, and I thank you for spending so much time with me. I'm planning on staying one more night. Would it be possible for me to come back tomorrow evening? I'd like to take you out for a meal and continue our conversation, if that's okay with you," I said.

"Yes, that would be really nice, thanks," Mia replied.

"I have a lot to think about in the meantime."

She stood up slowly and walked me to the door. She looked up at me, smiled and simply said, "Until we meet again."

I walked down to the promenade and watched the sea for a while. There was no one in sight. The night was still with the moon lighting the path before me and I breathed it all in.

CHAPTER FOUR

The seagulls woke me up a lot earlier than I would have liked. Hearing them made me feel so relaxed that I lay there thinking and dreaming, finding myself in the space between wakefulness and sleep. A carousel of images passed in front of my eyes and for a while, I enjoyed the scenery, even though I couldn't quite make out what I was seeing. I felt good. I went out and had a marvelous fry-up of a breakfast then headed for Land's End. I had hours to go before my meeting with Mia that night. I parked in a small, muddy car park off the beaten track. I had no desire to enter the glossy theme park which dominated this most south-westerly point of the British Isles. I'd brought no walking boots with me but the weather was fine. I started walking along the coastal path which was flanked with bright yellow gorse.

The day was warm and sunny. I enjoyed the solitude as I basked in the mild scent of coconut in the air and the deep radiant blue-green of the sea - Cornish colors in Cornish light. Then the weather turned. There was a chill in the air and the drops of rain soon turned into a heavy downpour. Trying to make my way back to the car, I felt myself becoming angrier and angrier until I was as enraged as the landscape around me. And just like the weather, this rage seemed to have arrived out of nowhere.

While as the night before had been magical, and the following morning an afterglow, the afternoon now turned on me so suddenly and unexpectedly that I was fighting not only the demons of nature but also those that lie in wait to feed off our vulnerabilities. I felt utterly helpless and devoid of understanding. Even if there had been a helping hand reaching out, metaphorical or real, I wouldn't have noticed. I was too deep in anger and doubt. But anger about what? My head ached from the myriad of questions that I was yet unable to formulate let alone find the answers to.

Why had I come to Penzance? So what if I had 'an experience'? I was suddenly sure there would be a logical explanation although I actually couldn't think of one. And even if there weren't, what's the big deal? What did any of this have to do with me? So what if I had once been this extraordinary tribal leader – I wasn't in this life. People get off on past lives as a way not to face the present. Perhaps they used it as an excuse for not facing reality. As for the crystal skulls, well, the experts say they have tool marks on them – relatively modern tool marks. They must all be fakes, even the one in my museum. That's got to be a fake too. It can't be an ancient artifact as Mia believed it to be. Suddenly, I was sure they were all fakes. Everybody with credibility said so. I felt as if I had fallen into a trap. Was it because I found Mia attractive? Was this the only way I knew how to make contact with a woman? Ever since Heather walked out on me, nothing had gone right. And that piece I wrote… was it really that special? Writers always talk about being touched by the divine – they like to call it poetry in prose.

I had indeed been touched by something powerful that I now wanted to brush aside. It had spoken to me and softly reached out much like a caress. It didn't look or feel like anything I thought a mystical experience ought to. I had no reference or perhaps, I thought it should have been more like the burning bush type of phenomenon. You see, there was this irritation inside of me; I don't know what else to call it. And it had erupted. I realized it had always been there, but there are so many different tricks for avoidance. Work is one of them. No wonder the statistics are so high for people who retire and then have a heart attack! They've spent their whole lives avoiding themselves. When there is finally time to breathe, to relax into themselves, they don't like what they see or are afraid of what they might see. Please don't get me wrong, there's nothing wrong with work. You can replace 'work' with anything that takes you away from yourself. Most don't have the luxury or the inclination if they do, to delve into their psyche. Let's face it; it's a difficult thing to do. It may be exciting; it may be thought-provoking; it may even be illuminating but it can be extremely unpleasant. To get to the beauty, there is a lot of ugliness to wade through. Very few have the courage to face their demons willingly. It's so much easier to blame others or stay in denial rather than take responsibility for the mishaps of our lives.

When I got back to The Blue Diamond, I had a long soak in the tub and several shots of whisky. I should have cancelled, not seen Mia that night. I was going through some sort of an evaluation and I needed to be alone. I'm not good with feelings but I hate cancelling even more. If I say I'm going to be somewhere, then you can count on me to show up because, after all, I am a responsible person.

We had arranged to meet at the Pelican. Mia said she wanted a fish pie, that she's never had one in America and that no one knows how to make it the way the Cornish do. And the Pelican happens to make really good fish pie. That was fine by me; I could use another drink. I enjoy my single malt but it's not an everyday occurrence. Today I needed the support of Bacchus himself.

She walked in so sure of herself, and yet seemed so small when I stood up to greet her. Mia is of average height for a woman, but I guess I'm the tall and lanky type. I usually have to look down at people which has always made me feel awkward, but now it made me feel confident. She looked up at me and had a quizzical expression on her face which instantly made me feel insecure.

"Hi, Eliot. Are you all right?" She asked.

"Yes, I'm fine." I knew that I was no longer present, that I was somewhere else; only present enough to follow along in conversation. What's that saying, 'the lights are on but nobody's home'? It was something like that.

"You don't look it. What's happened?"

"Mia, I'm quite well, really. I just got caught in that rainstorm earlier, and I got soaked."

She didn't say anything then, but looked at the menu.

"Thought you knew what you were going to have for your tea." I said, almost challenging her.

"I do, but I want to look all the same. What are you going to have?"

"Um, don't know yet. I'm not that hungry."

Her gaze grew intense. "Eliot, what's the matter? You seem strange."

"Guess I'm just tired." I sounded like an insolent teenager.

If I'd had time to think about what was happening, if I'd had time to turn the lights back on, I would have paid attention to the damage I was causing but I didn't. I was so confused.

"You know, I had a very nice time yesterday and I didn't realize we would talk for so long. Thanks for staying up late." Mia said.

I smiled, a genuine smile, but my insecurities had taken on a life of their own.

"What do you think about all of the new findings the scientists have come up with?" I asked. "That the crystal skulls in museums and private collections are fakes because they have tool marks on them?"

"Well, I find it very interesting, fascinating actually, how the scientific community always wants to discredit. There is always someone out there wanting to prove that there is no such thing as mystery and magic. Just because some crystal skulls have been carved and have tools marks does not take away from the fact that they have power. It's what the skull said to me that day and what I conveyed to you. The crystal skulls are to be used as tools for transformation; they are working tools. It also depends upon the people who carved them and the level of power available to transmit into the crystal. Scientists are only looking at a certain time period. They say because some have tool marks, it means they can't be ancient and that somebody planted these skulls in a particular location, like an ancient burial site as a hoax, or something like that. Maybe that's true for some, maybe not. Scientists are only looking at our more recent, ancient past for the answers. But what about beyond that time period - way beyond - where we have no scientific evidence whatsoever, and nothing's been discovered yet. You can only use theories on the facts that are laid out in front of you; therefore, there's no room for other possibilities."

"Well, you have a point, Mia. I don't know. Right now, I don't know anything. When I found out about the tool marks I made up my mind, even though I later discovered that the one in my museum didn't actually have any. Right then and there, I discarded the notion that this skull or any other had any powers, not that I had believed it in the first place...but somewhere in the back of your mind, you leave a speck of room for the possibility. Then when you find out that there really isn't any mystery, well, you feel a sense of satisfaction at being able to discredit the 'believers'. That little insignificant you can take the light out of someone's eyes, in a sense, makes you feel powerful. It's as if your ego smiles and says, 'I did that; it was my job to do that.' At the same time, if I'm really honest, you can't help but feel disappointed because you did want to believe there are supernatural powers that guide us."

"I think I know what you mean," Mia said. "Of course, a lot of those crystal skulls were carved in the 19th century or whenever it is that the scientists have suggested. And contemporary crystal skulls are everywhere now."

"I think I understand….," I said, my thoughts trailing off into multiple possibilities.

Our dinner had arrived. I had ordered the pie, forgetting that I don't like cream sauces. I picked at my food and drank several glasses of the Chardonnay I had ordered for us.

"Other crystal skulls including the one in the British Museum, truly are ancient, carved and encoded long ago with the knowledge of our ancestry - certainly long before the Mayans or Aztecs. What I'm trying to say is that some of the crystal skulls were from Atlantis," Mia said.

She sipped her wine and waited for my response, but at the mention of Atlantis; my stomach lurched, and my heart skipped a beat. While as before I was in an awful mood, I now found myself carrying emotions I didn't even know I had. Fear gripped me.

"I don't mean to pry, Eliot, but something's clearly troubling you. What is it?"

I mopped my brow with my napkin. "I'm not feeling very well. I think I have to go. I'm terribly sorry."

I took out a wad of money and almost threw it at the waitress as she walked past and said, "Please take care of her, whatever she wants."

All I knew was that I had to get out of there. The late autumn breeze helped clear my head a bit, but I just wanted to go home. I had way too much to drink and felt so queasy that I knew I couldn't leave as much as I wanted to. I went back to the hotel and slept it off as best as I could.

❧

I woke in a sweat, nauseous and hungry at the same time. I noticed a kettle in my room and made myself a cup of tea. Sitting up in bed, I stared out at the deep indigo of the sea. It looked pretty much how I felt – rough. I blamed it on the drink and lack of food, but deep inside, I knew there was a lot more to it than that.

Why had she come back into my life? Why? I was doing perfectly fine. The inadequacies I have felt were easily taken care of by suppression and false smiles. You deal; everyone deals with their own insecurities. No man's without them. Some just wear the façade better than others but no one is immune. You work hard and do the best you can. If by chance, you happen to meet the love of your life, then all the better for you. In the meantime, you get on with it. Life has its charm and pleasures, so enjoy them wherever they may fall. I have traveled, and I love my work at the museum. I was luckier than most, I concluded.

Who is she anyway, this Mia woman? Why has she come and disturbed my sleep, my peace, my equilibrium? And what did she want with me, a blood sacrifice?

I got dressed and stood in front of the window. 'Please help me; I don't know what's happening to me,' I said out loud to anyone that would listen.

Silence. Was I really expecting another voice? But I waited all the same. I just needed some answers, no, it wasn't answers – it was more than that. I wanted forgiveness, although I didn't know why.

❧

The next morning, I drove back up to London at break-neck speed with the windows rolled down and music blaring. I had brought a large black and white photo of the skull that the museum had recently taken, to give to Mia, but had forgotten to give it to her. It was in a pocket folder lying on the passenger seat. I was so pleased when I parked outside of my house and got out of the car that I inadvertently slammed the door a little too abruptly. The impact made the folder slide down beneath the seat and out of sight

CHAPTER FIVE

The weeks went by, and I immersed myself in work. I was too busy to think about the events that had occurred or at least that was the excuse I gave myself. I wasn't expecting to receive the phone call that came.

"Hello, Eliot. We haven't spoken in a long time." I paused for a second because I recognized the voice, but I couldn't quite place it.

"It's Drew Curtain from the Natural History Institute," he continued.

"Yes, of course! Hello, Drew. How are things with you?" I said.

"Good, good. Listen, I sent you a couple of emails and haven't heard back. I know how it is with emails; they seem to breed the way rabbits do," he chuckled. "So, I thought I'd contact you the old fashioned way."

"Sorry, Drew, I've been up to my eyeballs with a new exhibition, and I just haven't had the time to get back to you. What was it that you wanted to discuss?"

"The crystal skull. Would you be willing to loan it to us? We've recently acquired another skull and wanted to do extensive research on the two in our possession, yours at the British Museum, and two that are in private collections." I didn't say anything so he continued.

"Ever since that movie came out about crystal skulls, it's like people are coming out of the woodwork with them. Of course they're all fakes, but we really need to have proof. You know how people are."

"Sure, sure," I mumbled in agreement. "'I'll take it out of the display and send it to you. Give me a couple of weeks to get the paperwork done, and it's all yours."

"Great, thanks Eliot - looking forward to seeing Skully again. Always a pleasure doing business with you." He chuckled again as if what he had just said was exceptionally humorous. I knew he was referring to some television character, that I vaguely remembered, but I brushed it aside.

"Sure, sure," I said, not knowing what to say to him.

The minute I hung up the phone I was on to it. I had my assistant start the paperwork, and when the time came for the skull to be shipped to the Natural History Institute, I let my colleagues handle it all. I, of course, was too busy.

Months passed, and I became increasingly unhappy. Although I did not understand this at the time, I was grieving the discovery I had lost almost a breath after I had made it – the light I'd been searching for all my life; that I had so readily extinguished. When the sun is out, you feel its warmth, and bask in it. When it shines too brightly, it feels uncomfortable so you look for the shade. I looked for the shade because I thought I would get burned somehow. I did not realize that you can never have too much light because you are a part of it. In order to avoid sunburn, all you need do is adapt to that which is around you and within you to be able to bask in its splendor all the more.

I am not a loner; I realize I may have given that impression; actually, I have a lot of friends and colleagues – from all over the world. There's always someone to go out with, something to do, something to distract your mind. I had even started dating again. Her name was Tina, and we met at a charity event for the museum library. She was the event planner. She'd caught my eye instantly: tall, good looking, professional. A blond English rose, yet with more than a hint of Hollywood. She was someone any man would feel good about being seen with. She was witty, reliable and down to earth in a conventional sort of way. But something was missing between us, and I held myself back, not only from Tina but the world at large. Self-contained as I usually am, I could feel the seams of my self-imposed confinement slowly tearing to where I was hanging on by threads, although the suit appeared to still be intact. I knew I needed to talk to someone about my experiences, and I knew who that someone should be. Stephen would understand. It was he, after all, who had taken me to see Margaret in the first place.

I met Stephen back in university when we were both studying anthropology. He was now a professor. Although he was a few years older than I, he looked years younger. He had this youthfulness about him. Women seemed to love him, that is, except for Heather. He just had this way with women. He could speak their language, talk about the most mundane things with them like clothes and even make-up, and then engage in profound conversations. His appearance fooled you. He had dark, closely cropped hair, almost like an army officer, with different earrings in each of his ears. His clothes were a mixture of expensive and exotic. He also had no issues with wearing magenta. Today he had on a plain white cotton pirate type of a shirt paired with colorful Guatemalan striped trousers. Interestingly enough, the whole package suited him.

We arranged to meet on the South Bank. It was late afternoon in August, and stifling hot. I was sitting outside the British Film Institute overlooking the second-hand book stalls just in front of the river. The place was teeming with tourists, and I had to wait for ages for my coffee. The heat, the tourists, and the noise irritated me, but I also knew I was simply frightened to expose my vulnerabilities and share the experiences I had tried to bury. Yet I was looking forward to my time with Stephen, an intelligent and gifted man, the rare combination of a good listener and an excellent storyteller. The conversations I had shared with him in the past had not been unlike those with Mia, filled with wonder and possibilities and never confined to the ordinary. He led a fascinating life. And so I knew that I could reveal what had transpired with Mia and the skull. I don't know why I hadn't thought of him before.

"Hey, Sherlock," he shouted, as he came up riding his bike. He liked saying 'hey' instead of 'hi', intent on sounding as if he were from California instead of London.

"Stephen, my friend, it's good to see you," I said, smiling back at him. I hadn't been called Sherlock in a long time. It was the nickname I'd acquired back at Uni. It seems that I had the highest marks in archaeology class, so I earned the moniker as a result.

We got a couple of beers and a bite to eat. I started telling Stephen about Tina, which had nothing whatsoever to do with why I had wanted to see him.

"Not bad, not bad at all. Do you realize that she looks a lot like Heather?" Stephen said as I showed him a photograph on my phone.

"I hadn't noticed," I said. And in truth, I hadn't.

"Tall, blond, even the same expression. She's not got Heather's cruel streak though. Trust me, I can tell," Stephen said.

"I don't doubt you when it comes to women, Stephen," I said.

"So why does it sound like you're not all that taken with her?" he asked.

I took a deep sigh, and practically without pausing, breathed out the whole story of how I met Mia, my experience with the skull, my visit to Penzance, and basically everything else that had happened to me since that fateful evening at the museum. By the time I finished, I was famished. I'd been speaking, not eating, and Stephen just sat there staring at me wide eyed.

"Man, Sherlock, what a story!" Stephen breathed. "How long ago did all of this happen?"

"Almost a year ago."

"Are you kidding me? You've not been in touch with this woman for all that time? What in God's name are you afraid of?

"Please, Stephen, I feel bad enough as it is. I've been so busy with that new exhibition and my relationship with

Tina that I just haven't had time to think about any of this."

"Okay, let's get back to your relationship with Tina for a moment. She's a nice looking woman, a bit straight-laced, even if the lace is fine. But, Eliot, don't you see you're choosing to be with yet another woman that is safe and predictable? One who will never challenge you on what really matters? Tina's never going to fundamentally get who you are. You're a soulful man. I always knew that about you. Maybe most people can't see past your professional sophisticated manner – even your 'do-gooding' ways. But I can and always have. I've seen you at your best, Eliot, and even at your worst. But I know that the reason you studied anthropology was because you wanted to know what's underneath the surface of man's humanity and inhumanity - all of it. Remember, I've read your papers. A soulful man needs a soulful woman."

He smiled then, compassionately. He rarely addressed me as Eliot, so I knew what he was conveying was important, and I needed to hear it, even if I was shifting uncomfortably in my seat. I did my best to sit there patiently taking it all in. There wasn't any point in trying to defend Tina or the relationship. I knew he was speaking the truth, but I had already committed myself to Tina.

"Look, man, I'm not having a go, Eliot; really, I'm just trying to stir your juices. Put some fire under you. And the little fire that is there, you keep pissing on it, trying to put it out." Ever the gent, Stephen had pulled his chair closer to me and lowered his voice so as not to upset the tourists with his outburst.

I was about to interject, but Stephen had more to say.

"The beauty of this kind of magic, Sherlock, is that you don't have any of the head details. All you know is that there's a force, like a destiny, pulling you towards it. And I can imagine how hard that must be for you to not be able to define what this is, you know, label it in big black bold letters. You are on the edge of something, and it might feel like you're being pulled in the opposite direction of where you think you're headed. But really, you're not going to fall off a cliff. The world is round, Sherlock, not flat; you're not going to fall off."

"Okay, okay. I get it." This close to him it was impossible to hide my growing discomfort. He leaned back, put on his finest professor pose and continued to lay into me.

"No, Eliot, I don't think you do – get it. Most people aren't given the opportunity to do something," he paused, but not the sort of pause that invited interruption, "something really big - unless some tragedy occurs. If things are going smoothly, we mostly just sit back and take it easy. We all do because we are all inherently lazy. Given the right opportunity, however, we can move beyond our own little worlds and do whatever it takes to be of service. You're driving along and you see a car wreck, the person in front of you jumps out of his car and does whatever he can to help the injured driver knowing that the car may blow up at any second. When asked about his bravery, he says that he wasn't thinking about himself, he just wanted to help that person."

"Yes," I interrupted, "he lived up to his greatness and that will carry him and all those who witnessed the brave deed for a long time to come." I knew that's what Stephen wanted to hear so I played along and said it. But in my mind's eye I saw the man being blown to smithereens along with the car, the driver and his precious service to humanity. If Stephen did pick up on my doubts, he chose to ignore them.

"That's just my point, Eliot; you've been told about your past life - as a tribal leader, no less, and you've even had a 'visitation', from a priceless ancient relic - a crystal skull. To top it off, you've met this remarkable woman who knows a lot about this stuff and even shared with you some of what she knows. You may not yet understand what this is all about, but it's out there somewhere and now you have something to reach for. Allow for it to unfold. You've called this into your life, you know."

Stephen continued without pausing.

"The way you tell that story...you just light up! I could feel the excitement radiating off of you. And to think that you'd only met this woman for a few hours before going down to Cornwall a couple of days later and spending a whole evening staying up until the wee hours talking. That's more my style than yours, Sherlock. Well, I would have taken it a bit further, but, you get the gist. You felt so comfortable with her that you would do that, a complete stranger. And even more remarkable is that she would welcome you into her home and share some of her deep mystical experiences. Let me tell you, man, shamans and people of that type don't do that. They keep that kind of stuff pretty much to themselves - unless you're worthy somehow. So what does that say about you? You've met this woman who can help you uncover your role in all of this and help you find your greatness. Isn't that amazing?"

"Well, when you put it like that...." His enthusiasm was catching now and had indeed made me forget my unease.

"Of course, Sherlock! What I wouldn't give for an event like that in my life. I've gone to shamans, mediums, sweat lodges - you name it. I've never come close to what you've experienced. Most people are out there searching their whole lives to glimpse something out of the ordinary. Why do you think there are so many movies out there about UFOs and other worlds?"

I shrugged, not really knowing what to say.

"Because, dear Sherlock, we need to know that there is a bigger truth behind all the little truths we see and seemingly understand. We want to FEEL; we want to remember that we were once great and that we can still be." By now, Stephen was almost shouting in his excitement to get his point across. Both of us had forgotten that we were actually in a public place. He was right, of course. Our lives – this world and our place in it – are so much bigger and brighter than we could ever imagine. All we need do is allow the wonder in, take it inside of us with each new breath. When you do there is no room for confinement, the stays loosen and through the cracks the light pours in.

"Get out there, Sherlock, and go for it! What the hell are you waiting for?"

∽❧∾

Speaking to Stephen helped a great deal, but I didn't quite know where to take it all from there. I was embarrassed at never having called Mia after the episode at the restaurant. But at least now Mia and my experience with the skull wasn't left somewhere in a dark closet of my mind. It was now more in the hallway leading up to the living room. Even so, I still went about my life pretty much as normal. By this time, Tina and I were already discussing our future together. Or more to the point, she was doing the talking, and I was doing the listening. She was ready to take our relationship to the next level with a big shiny bling of a ring that would seal our commitment.

We were on our way to do just that, to look at engagement rings. She didn't like surprises. She didn't want to leave it to me to pick something she might not like. That's why we were on our way to the jeweler's that day. It all felt so rehearsed, not at all what I would have wanted; but she was bubbling with excitement and I wanted to make her happy.

Traffic was moving at a snail's pace and I was constantly shifting gears from first to second and back. I was just about to change into third when out of nowhere a motorcycle weaved in front of me and I had to slam on the brakes. No one was hurt. I turned to see if Tina was alright and, swearing under my breath, drove off again. That was when Tina noticed a folder at her feet and reached down to pick it up. It must have become dislodged when the car jerked to a halt.

"What's this?" she asked, opening the folder.

"No idea," I replied. But the minute I uttered those two words, I knew what it was and felt suddenly quite vulnerable – and protective.

"Oh, it's nothing, just leave it. I'll deal with that later."

"But what is it? It was stuck underneath my seat"

Tina opened the folder and took a look at the photo of the skull. "Oh, yuck, a skull! It's not yet Halloween is it?"

No doubt she thought she was being funny waving the picture at me. But hearing her make fun of the skull really upset me. "Put that back. That has nothing to do with you." My tone was harsh, and I think I was actually shouting at her.

"Of course it has nothing to do with me. But why are you speaking to me like that? What's wrong with you? How dare you speak to me like that!" She returned the picture to the folder and put it back on the floor in front of her. She did not want to hold it in her lap. Tina just sat there with arms crossed, fuming as the car once again slowed to a halt.

"I'm sorry, Tina, but it's called a crystal skull, and I think it's remarkably beautiful. In fact, I think it's one of the most extraordinary artifacts I have ever come across."

"Really! Extraordinary or not, you do not talk to me like that, Eliot, ever. Anthropologists, you're all crazy people. CRAZY PEOPLE."

I didn't say anything, but I felt myself getting pretty irritated. In an instant, I saw what my life would be like with Tina in the years to come. We would have a couple of kids - good kids. There would be weekend parties with our 'professional' friends, trips abroad. The kids would hold us together, and they would be the focus of our conversations. Once they left home, there would be nothing for us to talk about or share. The part of me that longed to be touched with wildness and wonder could never be reached because she would not know what to look for or how to draw it out of me. Not that it was her duty to draw that out of me rather, I couldn't reach down inside and pull it out and expose it; it just didn't fit in that world. Tina was lovely and she was kind, but we were not meant to journey through life together.

What the soul desires most, I believe, is authenticity; an authenticity that carries both the light and dark aspects to be examined and understood. I drove Tina back home, and we said goodbye that day.

❧

This time I didn't forget about the folder. I took it home with me, placed it on the kitchen table and made myself some tea. I opened it tenderly as if inside lay something precious. I was focusing on the picture of the skull once again wondering about its beauty, the perfection of the curves, the clarity of the crystal. I felt myself being pulled into the photograph, or maybe it was that the skull pulled itself out of the photograph to meet me. This all happened so quickly that

I could only make sense of it in hindsight. Mystical experiences happen fast for the simple reason that your mind does not have time to engage. If it did, the experience could not happen. The mind, you see, would have wanted center stage, to be the star of a part that does not belong to it. And the essence of the experience would be left somewhere backstage, lost in the shadows of mind's delight with only an imprint of what might have been.

I don't know how long I remained in this place between worlds. I was conscious of sitting at my kitchen table, and I could smell the aroma of Earl Grey tea. The dogs next door were barking, and my neighbor scolded them. It was familiar and had the effect of keeping me grounded in that place and time. And yet, I was journeying to another place and time.

I hadn't far to go, not in the physical sense. I was still in the same kitchen, but it was mine and Heather's. We had been quarrelling about something insignificant, and we were now making up. She stood on a low wooden stool. She was 5'10", tall for a woman, but she wanted to be exactly at eye level with me and the stool provided her another five inches. We held each other, and I silently called on the powers that be to let her stay with me because the moment before I heard a voice that had said, 'It's time, Eliot.' I knew what that meant without consciously knowing. They wanted me to redeem myself, fulfill my destiny, but I loving Heather so much, wanted to hold on to her – to us – to the life I had grown into. I was happy and fulfilled in my love for her; that was all I needed. So I begged them for more time.

It was granted. I had another year, I was told. Then they faded, departed out of my consciousness and out of my life. Five years later, the memory of that evening surfaced. I had not even known then that I had my own connection to the crystal skulls or that it was them that had spoken to me that day. I also knew that I had known Mia lifetime after lifetime, that we were connected in the most profound way and I had stood by her side when she encoded the skull with knowledge in that place beyond time. It came back to me as in a dream.

Exactly one year later to the day, Heather left me for another. It had to be that way. I can see that now because I would never have left her. I lost a lot that day, the family I never had but always dreamt of. But now sitting at my kitchen table, I understood things differently. I saw that I had grieved far too long. There were those who would have opened their hearts to me but I, bearing a torch, could only see the flame I carried that blinded the light that surrounded me. We carry our wounds like this, I believe.

If we can only trust that there is a divine plan for us all, that we are not simply at the mercy of circumstance.

That was what was revealed to me that evening. In order for me to fulfill my destiny with my ancient past, I had to heal my most recent one. I also knew that saying goodbye to Tina was the catalyst for this to happen. I realized that I had closed my heart and in order to heal my deepest wounds, I needed an open heart. Healing isn't linear. When a healing experience happens, it's because at that moment that's what you are ready to let go of. 'I am ready' is what

I'd said to the skull. A deep purple light hit me and poured over me, as if I were being anointed with the purest of love in my heart, in the center of my forehead and in my solar plexus – three points of divine light that spread and filled me with an exquisite joy unlike any I had ever before experienced. Not only did I feel more than I thought possible, but I was blessed and touched by a power most beautiful and divine.

I came back to myself still holding the photo. I reached for my tea but it was cold. It didn't matter; I would make another. For once I didn't try to analyze; I was too tired for that anyway. I slept and when I woke, I knew that I was ready to make that call.

CHAPTER SIX

I didn't end up making that phone call after all. Instead, I took time off work and headed down to Penzance. I didn't know for sure if Mia would be there, but I took the chance. I wanted to talk to her in person. I made my reservations at The Blue Diamond, like the last time. This time though, it felt different. There was no apprehension. I let my heart guide me and my mind retreated, knowing that this time, it had no choice but to relent.

I took my time driving down. I had taken a couple of days off from work and felt as if I had all the time in the world. So I waited for the opportune moment to call in on Mia, which happened to be the following morning. It was the end of October, sunny but cold. The wind had a bite to it, as a reminder that winter would soon be upon us. I stopped at a bakery along the way and bought some croissants and pastries which I carried in a shopping bag. The folder with the photo of the skull nestled underneath my arm. As I approached, I could see that the front door to Mia's house was wide open. I opened the gate cautiously, slowly walked to the door and laid the bag down at my side. I wasn't quite sure whether I should shout, knock or ring the doorbell. I stood there waiting for the right cue when I saw Mia walking down the stairs. For a second I got to observe her before she noticed me. She had a blue and white scarf tied around her hair and wore a pair of baggy trousers and an old gray sweater. She looked like she had stepped right out of 1940's wartime England. She looked up and stopped, her right leg was in mid-air, as if it didn't know whether to take that next step down. There was enough of a distance between us, so I spoke loudly. I dared not cross the threshold until invited.

"Hello, old friend," I said. Mimicking what the skull had said to her that very first time. This felt like a new beginning, so I thought my greeting was somehow appropriate. "I was in the neighborhood and saw that your front door was open."

She walked down slowly and said, "Would you mind closing the door behind you? I was only airing the place."

I did as I was told and stood there. I had the folder of the skull with me and held on to it. I was thankful for that because I don't think I would have quite known what to do with my arms. Mia was still on the stairwell. I didn't know what was going through her mind. By this time she had come down a few more steps, enough so that she could be at eye level with me. And then she looked right into me. It is extraordinary just how much communication goes on without words. I looked at her sheepishly - please forgive me was what I tried to convey. At first, she would not relent. She looked down and moved her eyes to the right, not focusing on anything in particular, as though she were deep in thought. I kept my gaze on her and would not let go.

Look at me was what I was saying. It took only a second for her to shift her gaze straight back, but it felt much longer. I got that it wasn't that she didn't want to forgive me; rather that forgiveness is a process which takes time. So I came straight to the point.

"You cast your pearls and I was a pig for not contacting you again. But please know that it had nothing to do with you. I can't tell you how much I've enjoyed every minute that I've spent with you. I knew that we had a connection but I didn't know what it was and I was confused by it; it didn't seem to fit in with my life as I was leading it. I had to go away to figure it out, even though I didn't even know that I had to go away to figure it out. Or even that it would take so long to get back in touch with you. I guess I'm a slow learner."

"What am I going to do with you?" Mia said, half smiling, walking down the stairs. She turned around, waved her arm at me and simply said, "Come in."

The place smelled clean, of orange oil furniture polish with just a hint of incense lingering in the background. I almost tripped over the cord of the Hoover that was still connected to the socket.

She caught the shopping bag as I let go of it and held on to the back of an armchair so as to keep my balance. The folder went flying across the room.

"I've been housecleaning," she simply said.

"And I've been shopping for pastries."

We both started laughing as Mia went to pick up the folder. It had landed on the floor across the room.

That folder sure has a lot of energy, I thought to myself, chuckling. She was about to return it to me when I said, "No, please, it's for you. I meant to give this to you a long time ago." Opening it, she smiled and said, "Thank you, it's beautiful!" She placed the photo of the skull on the mantel above the fireplace.

"Should I go and put the kettle on?" I asked, feeling quite brave now.

"I'm expecting company at lunch time," she said.

"You are? I'm so sorry to intrude. I just took a chance…"

"No, it's all right, really. It's Margaret; she's coming over from Lamorna for lunch. I'm sure she'd be delighted to see you," Mia said, "but there'll be time for us to catch up before."

A few moments later, we were in her kitchen with coffee and croissants. And just like the last time, the more serious topics of conversation were put on hold. It was as if we were simply two ordinary people getting reacquainted with one another.

⚜

I don't know why I was nervous at the prospect of meeting Margaret again but when she arrived promptly at noon with Ajax, her little Chihuahua and Jack Russell mix of a dog, I saw I needn't have bothered.

"Hi Margaret. Hi Ajax," I heard Mia say in the hall. "I have an unexpected visitor who will be joining us for lunch."

"Oh, really? I love surprises!" I heard Margaret say.

Ajax ran to find me and greeted me with much enthusiasm. It took a couple of minutes for them to follow Ajax in. They were speaking in hushed voices I noticed.

"I see you've already met Ajax," Margaret said as she approached me and drew me to her for a hug.

"Good to see you, Eliot, it's been a long time. I would have recognized you though, I never forget a face."

"Nice to see you too, Margaret." I replied. "And nice to meet Ajax." At the mention of his name, Ajax gave a little wiggle. He was very much a part of the conversation.

"Please, Margaret, sit down and talk with Eliot while I go and prepare lunch."

"All right, if you insist," she said.

Margaret and Ajax were a sight to behold both wearing matching, shiny red scarves. Margaret, I vaguely remembered, loved the color red, and it suited her. She had short stylish white hair and still wore the bright crimson lipstick that had been her trademark her entire life. Her face was quite lined; it looked like a treasure map to me, every wrinkle a timeline, a clue to her life. Her eyes were of a deep blue-green, and they like the red lips, matched her personality perfectly. Everything about Margaret said 'vibrant'.

"Come and sit by me, Eliot," she said and motioned for me to sit next to her. I must have been staring at Mia when she headed for the kitchen because Margaret whispered to me.

"Just don't put her on a pedestal. Although she belongs on one, she doesn't need it, and she won't appreciate it."

I looked up at her quizzically. Margaret continued.

"You heard me," she said, a bit stern, making me feel like an overgrown schoolboy. She continued, "It will take some time for the both of you to become used to being around each other again and get to grips with all that energy that is zapping between you. The two of you are very powerful people in your own right. You need to be in your power as much as she does. So take your time, Eliot. She needs as much time as you do to get used to being with you. It's like the two of you have to dance around and do a little bit of a jig first before you can tango. Lucky for both of you I'm here. Hahahaha!"

Margaret always seemed to laugh at her own jokes. Ajax gave a little bark as if he were in agreement.

Dumfounded, I didn't know quite what to say, so I kept silent. Margaret ignored my surprise.

"It wasn't easy for her not hearing from you in all that time, you know." Margaret said.

"I'm sorry. I didn't mean to hurt her in any way," I replied.

"I know you didn't and so did she. She *is* psychic, remember. However, it's difficult when the person you've been waiting for your whole life suddenly appears and then promptly leaves just when you were getting acquainted. It's not like she could have a relationship with just anyone. It would have to be with someone very special – someone who can know and respect what Mia is about."

I nodded at Margaret in agreement.

"You two have shared so many lifetimes together, I can see them weaving in and out of your auras. It's quite fascinating how connected you are to each other. And now you have chosen to meet up once again, to be together for this very special time on planet earth."

"And why is that?" I asked.

"Why? To assist humanity, of course – and also for your own personal self-empowerment."

To call Margaret direct would have been unfair to her. She had a way of getting to the point without having to go through any of the small talk one would expect from a person you'd only met once a long time ago. She intuitively knew how to talk to people in a manner appropriate to them. I respected that about her and knew that even though she had only just scratched the surface, the details would be revealed in time. When you were with Margaret, you had to step it up a pace or two in order to keep up. She was always open to questions, willing to explain anything, but she did not like to play games.

"Just allow it to unfold, Eliot," she said warmly. "For now, for today, be here with us and enjoy the company. You're with two wacky women and one crazy little dog. How can you not enjoy yourself? Maybe there's room in your museum to put us all on display."

Just then Mia walked in with a big smile on her face. She was happy Margaret and I had hit it off.

We sat down at the dinner table and had a simple lunch of pasta, salad and garlic bread. I was famished and ate more than both of them combined.

"Glad to see he's got an appetite," Margaret said.

"And I'm glad because that means he must like my cooking," Mia replied.

They were speaking to one another as if I weren't there. I looked down at Ajax who, up until that time, sat patiently waiting for a hand out and I, of course, willingly obliged.

"It must be the sea air," I said. "And your delicious cooking, too, Mia," I added quickly so as not to cause offense.

They looked at one another and began roaring with laughter.

"No, really it truly is delicious," I said smiling. I didn't want Mia to think that I was being polite when, in fact, I felt I was eating the most delicious meal I had ever tasted.

"And how did you get from being a 'normal' person to the person you are now, Margaret?" I asked in the midst of all this.

"Margaret was never normal, Eliot, so how could you ever think that?" Mia said when she had time to compose herself.

"What is this fascination you have with normalcy anyway, Eliot? Are any of us normal? Thank God we can't get into other people's heads - well, some of us can - but I mean, intentionally. Not a good idea," Margaret said, still laughing.

"Well, I am the curator of ethnography, after all, 'eth-no' refers to the study of man, of cultures, and 'graph' means to record. I'm trying to make sense of this in order to classify it for myself," I said, hopelessly defending myself. "How can I not be fascinated by the two of you, the dynamic duo?"

By this time, we'd had our coffee and the pastries I'd brought and settled back to the living room as Ajax wanted to be able to sit with us. The conversation turned and took on a more serious note.

"You know, Margaret really has always been so much fun. And she's had a great deal of tragedy in her life as well. Her daughter died of a terminal illness when she was two years old. She was her only child. That was long before I met her, but soon after, her husband left, unable to handle it."

I was stunned at hearing this. From the looks on their faces, I knew it showed.

"I'm so sorry, Margaret. I don't quite know what to say. That must have been awful."

There was a pause that felt a little uncomfortable, and then Margaret spoke.

"Yes, it was awful. That was a long time ago, Eliot. I went through a lot. And suffering brings us closer to Great Spirit, or whatever you want to name it. It doesn't just have to be through some dreadful tragedy like sickness, death and poverty but anything that takes us away from our center. If you have an easy life, in the sense that you have wealth and are healthy, and life hasn't thrown you a few good wrenches, then you manage to float along somehow. Unfortunately, most people don't have all that much empathy, unless they've experienced something similar."

"But how did you grow into the person that you are today? Mia told me about the effect you had on her when you and she first met, but how did your special abilities develop?" I asked.

"I think you romanticize what life is like for people like Margaret and me." Mia teased.

"Well, perhaps I do, a little. But I guess I'm interested in how you have opened yourselves up in a sense - to this world from where you came from."

"First of all," Margaret mused, "I think we all have special gifts to varying degrees. It's just that most of us haven't chosen to develop them. There are those of us who weren't given a choice, whose gifts are very much at the forefront of our lives – meant, of course, to be used for the benefit of others. Those gifts naturally open up when they're meant to, when the time is right. I, for instance, always knew that I was clairvoyant. Ever since I was little, I could see auras. I thought everyone could. I was fortunate in that I had parents who believed me. My mother was a bit fey herself."

She turned to Ajax, who was sitting next to her and began petting him.

"But I've had many difficulties, many self-induced. Did Mia tell you that I had been a drug addict?"

I was startled. Unsure, at first, if Margaret was joking, I could tell by the look on her face that she was not. I don't know why I should have been startled, actually. In that moment, I understood what Mia was trying to tell me only moments before about projection and romanticizing about another's life. It's easy for them, somehow, because they are special and gifted. Life hands them opportunities that don't normally present themselves to us ordinary folk. We view a person as they impress us in the moment, and rarely see what it took for them to get there.

I have never forgotten the line in *To Kill a Mockingbird* where Atticus tells his daughter Scout, 'You never really understand a person until you consider things from his point of view, until you climb into his skin and walk around in it.'[2]

We hear these sayings all the time which can be profound. But then we lose sight of them continuing to compare ourselves to others which can only lead to judgment and feelings of inadequacy. These are things we certainly don't need or deserve.

Margaret could see that I was quite taken aback by the revelation of her past and somehow sensed what I had been thinking.

"You know, Eliot, I think it's our birthright to manifest our soul's purpose. To open your heart and love with passion and compassion takes a lot of work in some ways and none at all in others." Margaret said.

"When we can recognize people for the qualities they possess, even if you only meet them for a moment, I think that recognition somehow strengthens who they are and you, as well. We are so connected to each other and when you hold someone in a negative light, what you're doing is

---

2   Lee, Harper, To Kill a Mockingbird, (New York, NY: HarperCollins, Publishers, Inc., 1960), 33

suppressing their energy in a very subtle way. Somehow; you are holding them back just as you are when you're critical of yourself. It's the same thing," Margaret concluded.

"I owe a lot of gratitude to Margaret," Mia said, looking directly at me. "I've kept myself hidden from most people, as well as from myself, for many years. I wasn't given the opportunity as a child to just be a child; I had too many responsibilities with caring for a sick mother. When you have to shoulder that burden too early in life, before you've even had a chance to grow into yourself, you start to feel as if your own needs are not worthy of expression. I used to have this children's book, with the most beautiful illustrations in it of fairies and gnomes and things like that. I could enter into the picture and it would come alive for me. That's when I knew that there was more to life than what was visible, that the intangible was just as real. That insight gave me strength and I built on it. Still, that wasn't enough to pull me out into the world. It wasn't until I met Margaret and she told me to 'claim my space' that I really started to grow. Do you remember that, Margaret?"

"Yes, I do. Claiming space is a very important aspect in a person's life. Think of people you know that are larger than life. They walk into a room and everyone notices them; they have a big presence. Some are incredibly wonderful to be around while others are so obnoxious, always wanting attention. Their company can be so draining. Those people have claimed way too much space for themselves. They want attention, at any cost. Whether it's good or bad, they need to be noticed. Then there's the opposite – people who walk around meekly hoping not to be seen. They either don't want to be drawn out, or they don't feel they have a right to receive attention from anyone. They either think of themselves as not important enough or don't want anyone to notice how important they truly are."

Margaret paused, and I sat there quietly thinking about the category that I fell under and knew, of course, that I was the retiring type. I sighed then because I understood the difference between a naturally quiet person and one withdrawn into himself when what was required was really the opposite.

"Think how wonderful it is to live in balance, to claim and take the space that you need, the space that is yours," Margaret said, looking at me as if she had just read my thoughts. "It's when you claim your space that your prayers are answered. Did you know that?" Margaret asked.

"I guess I hadn't thought about it," I said.

"Well, think about it," Margaret continued. "If your energy is tiny, you don't feel worthy enough to have a presence that will hold who you are in this world. How do you expect the universe to provide what you're asking of it? The same is true when you take up so much space; there isn't any room for blessings to come in because you haven't made any room for them. You're so caught up in your own illusion of grandeur. So finding the correct balance that's perfect for you is of the utmost importance. It's incredibly subtle, this energy we put out into the world. Recognition of self is truly the key. That recognition is what's going to enable you to walk in this world with both feet firmly planted, leaving your mark without taking. The trick is to just allow the essence of who you are to carry itself along and experience the world you live in."

Margaret had a way of finishing off a discussion leaving me with more than enough food for thought.

"Excuse me, please," I said, getting up and going into the back garden. It was off the kitchen, an enclosed garden, nice and private. Although it was the end of October, there were plenty of flowers. I recognized the fuchsia bushes and the purple hydrangeas. A washing line had been strung up between the shed and the side of the house with laundry drying on it – all white, sheets and towels and things of that nature. I could smell the cleanness of it. They hung there swaying gently in the breeze, taking all the time in the world they needed to dry. I sat on the patio on one of those metal 'sweetheart' garden chairs, also painted white, rolling my cigarette. I noticed I smoked a lot more when I was around Mia, but I wasn't going to focus on that just yet. Instead, I enjoyed the moment, the smoke and all that whiteness."

I knew it was time for me to leave and when I got back inside, I told them just that.

"Thank you for such a lovely afternoon."

Margaret gave me a hug and said, "I was just talking to Mia, and have invited the both of you round to my place for dinner. Would you like that? You can go on a nice hike up to Land's End."

"That would be great!" I replied.

"Wonderful. I'll see you both tomorrow then. And be good to yourself, dear," she said. Sometimes she sounded so old-fashioned, like a genteel old lady. I could just picture her wearing a wool tartan skirt and plain beige-colored blouse buttoned right up to the collar. It always took me by surprise when she displayed that side of her character, and I loved her all the more for it.

Mia walked me to the door with Ajax following at her heels. I looked at her tenderly as she stood on tiptoes to give me a hug.

"Thank you, Mia. I'm so glad that I took a chance and came down."

"Me too," was all she said. She smiled and gently closed the door behind her.

CHAPTER SEVEN

Rosewood Cottage, as Margaret's place was called, was off the road that leads to Lamorna Cove. You had to walk down steps to get to it so that it had a sense of privacy that you would not expect from a house situated directly off the main road. Behind the cottage ran a stream surrounded by woodland. The seclusion and sound of the stream instantly gave the feeling of peacefulness and relaxation.

"I was told that there is a vortex here. That is one of the reasons why you can feel both peaceful and energized at the same time," Margaret said.

"A vortex?" I asked.

"Yes, I had some people with dowsing rods tell me that. The dowsing affirmed what I had already suspected. This is a powerful place, Eliot. Your thoughts and feelings get amplified here. That's what a vortex does. It carries energy and magnifies it, sending it out into the ethers, inner planes, the universe – call it what you will," Margaret said, waving her arms for effect.

We were sitting upstairs in the cottage looking out at the stream. Although the windows were closed, the sound of the stream could still be heard and the crackling of the fire only added to the beauty that surrounded us. I looked at Mia, who sat opposite on the sofa. She sat with her legs crossed yoga-style and looked regal even for one sitting in such a position. Mia had spoken of her aunt's artistic talent but I could see that Mia also was artistic. She loved to make her own clothes and had been designing the costumes for the local theatre company. She wore wide legged velvet green trousers and a black top with ruffles at the sleeves. She looked beautiful.

"I kept meaning to mention to you, Eliot, I really liked the photo of the skull that you gave to Mia. It seems that we had so much to talk about yesterday. Still, I can't believe I didn't slip it in somehow."

"Yes, I'm glad you like it," I said. Do you also work with the skulls the way Mia does?" I asked.

"Not exactly. I am not a channel of the crystal skulls but they do speak to me when they need to convey a message to Mia when she cannot seem to hear them. You know how it is - sometimes it's easier when somebody else tells you things than when you hear it for yourself. Occasionally, they have come to me and I can, of course, feel their presence and receive messages but I am not a guardian. Mia acts as a conduit of holding and transmitting the energy of the crystals skulls so that you can experience them for yourself, as I'm sure you're aware of by now," she said, with a twinkle in her eye. I grinned back at her and Ajax, who always seemed to know when to add his own opinion, gave a little bark as confirmation that we were all on the same page.

"You see, people can be scared of it and Mia's not. Most people are afraid of power and the ones that aren't usually don't really know what power is. And then of course, in our current culture the image of a skull is so often associated with negative things like death and poison. Few people understand the beauty of our bones — that they are the structure in which we are supported in the physical sense and metaphorically, with the skull as a fount of our spirituality."

Margaret rearranged the cushion supporting her back and put her feet up on the little footstool in front of her. Ajax took this as an invitation to jump onto her lap. Stroking his back, she continued.

"The skulls don't allow just anyone to tap into their power. There is absolutely no room for pretense here! Like a key that unlocks a door, your vibration can unlock the knowledge they carry. However, if your vibration is not in alignment, the key will simply not fit. That is the secret and the mystery of the crystal skulls. The power they possess will only be revealed to those of us who can withstand their vibrations or emanations. And all such knowledge must be used for the benefit of all. Since power may corrupt, you will only receive a little at a time, until it sits comfortably within you."

Margaret paused to take a quick breath, continuing where she'd left off.

"So Mia acts as a mirror, if you like, and in that way, enables you to see or feel the impressions of the skulls. Now we come to the interesting bit, Eliot. Are you paying attention?"

I couldn't have been paying any more attention. Outrageous as this all sounded, I knew in my heart that what Margaret was telling me was true. I understood that what I was being told was important and more relevant to my future than anything I had ever been told before.

Margaret grinned at my serious face and said, "You, Eliot, are also an initiate of the mysteries and are connected to Mia in the most profound way. It is my belief that you have come at this time to assist her in some very important rituals that will help heal particular imbalances of a transpersonal nature. In doing so, you will both be of service to this planet – to the collective consciousness – enabling humanity to open, receive and evolve into better human beings."

I looked over at Mia for confirmation and reassurance. She nodded, not by slightly bowing her head in the usual manner, but merely with her eyes. There was no embarrassment or shyness. Margaret had simply stated a fact.

"But how would Mia and I working together assist the whole of humanity?" I asked Margaret, attempting to make sense of it all.

"Because when you set your intention on working for the greater good you take on a transpersonal role, that is, you become all men and Mia, all women. You both act as ambassadors for humanity."

A warm silence fell around us then, with each of us wrapped in our own thoughts.

"Think about how all living creatures on this planet are affected by crystals. These crystalline structures are in the earth and in the very core of your being," Margaret said, "and crystal technology is prevalent everywhere – you need look no further than your own computer to know that this is so."

And without waiting for any signs of comprehension on my part, Margaret elaborated, "There is a natural filtering system for energies to travel down to earth. Positive or negative, it doesn't matter. We can all feel it although most of us aren't consciously aware."

I was riveted as she went on, "At this time, there are new frequencies that are being passed down to earth to activate the crystals on the planet and, in turn, awaken your own crystal body. When one shifts in consciousness and becomes aligned with one's inherent nature, then the positive energies will flow and multiply as light attracts light. This will create new forms of energy that have not existed on this planet before."

Margaret paused to look at Mia and me, making sure that we were keeping up with her. We nodded in unison. Margaret beamed back at us and continued.

"It is, therefore, a very special time to be on earth. It's a time of transformation, a leap, if you will, into another phase in the development of mankind's evolution. Now then, you must understand that this growth in consciousness is very subtle but nevertheless dramatic because there is so much of it. The more you become aware of the vibrations that are around you, the more you will awaken."

She paused, suddenly glancing over at the bookcase, as if the books were speaking to her directly.

"The skulls are in a sense androgynous and you may experience them as either male or female or both at different times. Although they do come with more of a feminine vibration, as women have been misrepresented for centuries. A remembrance and resurgence of Her greatness is needed at this time for harmony and balance. That is why two people such as yourselves, who have worked on developing and balancing your anima and animus, can come together to assist humanity – as archetypes and as conduits for this energy to pass through."

We thought that she had finished but she had one more thing to say and it was addressed specifically to me.

"Eliot, whenever a distinction needs to be made, the skulls like to be referred to in the feminine."

Then she smiled and the conversation came to its natural end.

❦

There are special days you hold dear to your heart that you will remember for the rest of your life, not necessarily because they were pivotal but because you felt alive, nourished, and so in the moment. We don't realize how often we live life out of balance.

Being with these two women was really nourishing. They offered me different kinds of friendship. My mother died when I was a boy. My father had been despondent for years so my brother and I were left to fend for ourselves. When he finally remarried years later, I was already a grown man. Perhaps that was why the female of the species always seemed elusive, carrying something that I could never understand or be a part of in the familial sense.

Margaret broke the silence with an announcement that she would prepare our dinner and that Mia and I should go for a walk.

"Are you sure you don't want us to help make dinner, Margaret?" Mia asked.

"No, no, I've got it all under control. You know how much I like to cook. Go on, enjoy the walk and please take your time. I'm going to make a good old-fashioned roast chicken dinner and Yorkshire Pudding."

"Oh, Margaret, you're the best! My favorites." Mia, elated, looked like she was 12 years old.

We walked along the coastal path from Lamorna to Land's End. Although it was overcast and pretty cold, the air had a special something that made you want to go out and be in it. We stopped off at a pub for a pint and a packet of crisps and then headed back. It had taken us a good three hours.

"You know," I said to Mia, "I really do feel like I'm on holiday. It's nice coming down here when it's not overrun with holiday-makers. I can see why you like coming here off-season."

"The sea down here reminds me of Kali," Mia said, standing on top of the cliff looking outward.

"You mean the Hindu goddess?"

"Yes."

"Why exactly?"

"Because she destroys and then rebuilds. She removes the darkness and destroys demons."

"She's the one that wears the garland of skulls, isn't she?"

"Yes, that's her. But those skulls don't represent death. What she destroys are our own demons. And then we get to see the beauty. So she really isn't as dark as she appears to be," Mia said.

"Are you saying that she destroys the ego when we are willing to let go? And if we're not willing, she can seem fierce, ugly and definitely scary. I can see why you like her with the garland of skulls and all, but how does she remind you of the sea and, in particular, this one?"

"Well, for most people, "Mia explained, "this place isn't where you would come to make your fortune. There aren't that many jobs and if you're lucky to have one, the salaries are very low. For those who have been compelled to live down here from other parts of the country or if you're a foreigner like I am, it's like an initiation of sorts. You have to shed something in order to be accepted.

The sea brings stuff up – you can't hide from it. It can be fierce. Think of all the shipwrecks that have happened around here. But Kali brings blessings, too, and she renews. This is a fishing community as well; Newlyn down the road is still a busy working harbor. When the weather is warm enough to swim, you can feel her right beside you. That very physical sensation of being in the sea, while at the same time being in the company of Spirit is exhilarating beyond compare.

I believe that when you spend enough time down here, the sea stirs something in your psyche and whatever's hidden gets exposed somehow."

"Umm," I responded. "I really wouldn't know about that. I don't think I've spent enough time down here yet. But I most definitely feel something. Exhilarating is a good word to describe it. Magnificent would be another. And I thought that was because of you and Margaret rather than the sea."

We laughed then, a good hearty laugh shared as old friends do.

"I was thinking about what you said about people not having much money. I guess you'd have to be creative. I can see that there are lots of artists down here."

"Yes, but I think it's not just creative in an artistic sense but about wanting to make a contribution, to share your gifts whatever they may be. People do all kinds of trades here. They help each other out in so many ways. Someone might grow organic vegetables in trade for carpentry. It's amazing. Of course money has its place, too, but when I look at these people and this land, I see abundance."

"You're right. It's a simple life and so natural and interesting at the same time. There's a lot going on down here. I can smell it." I replied.

Mia laughed. "You can smell it?"

"Well, yes, I have a nose for things."

"Ah, yes," was all she said.

We walked in silence for a good while and came upon an acquaintance of Mia's. We said our hello's and when they had passed us by, Mia started up the conversation.

"What I like is that when you meet someone here, you're never asked what you do. You are asked how you are and that's a big difference. That would never happen in America. In America, you are pretty much labeled by what you do. That's the first impression and for most people who aren't interested in looking any further, that's all that they see. It is rare for someone to get that what you do for a living may not have anything to do with who you are."

"Pity, that. Even in London, I guess we English are too polite for that. But I know that these parts of the country are different. When I came down to Cornwall with my friend, Stephen, all those years ago, we met some pretty interesting people. You've got plenty of witches and those that live off the beaten track, not only physically but on the fringes of society."

"Absolutely, that's what's so special. You are who you are."

"So, Mia, are you a good little witch or a bad one?"

"What do you think, Eliot?" Mia teased.

"Well, definitely good, but I can see something in there that could be pretty scary if unleashed, not unlike Kali, I guess."

We were joking with each other but there really was a truth in what I had said except there was nothing 'little' about Mia.

After our meal, we sat again in that comfortable room overlooking the brook. Margaret and Mia actually let me have a cigarette. I do like to smoke a couple in the evenings and I especially enjoy rolling the tobacco myself. The feel and the smell of it is a ritual all of its own.

So I sat there, rolling my cigarette, enjoying the pleasure of their company.

"I've been meaning to ask you this for some time," I said. "I keep getting that there's a difference between being a guardian or a priestess of the crystal skulls and someone simply in possession of them. Is that accurate?"

Margaret and Mia both nodded in agreement, so I continued.

"In my line of work, I have come across one or two people that have owned some really beautiful crystal skulls but when I think of them, and you, Mia, they certainly don't seem like guardians."

"That's because they're not," Margaret stated flatly. "See, you're right. You have to realize that being in possession of a crystal skull and being its guardian are two totally different things. When you are merely in possession of a skull, it's about acquiring a valuable object for personal pleasure or gain. A guardian's role, however, is to protect and preserve the knowledge contained *within* the skull. A guardian also does not have to physically 'own' a skull. You really can't 'own' a sacred object, as it belongs to the divinity from whence it came.

"And how can you tell the difference?" I asked.

"That's quite simple. The one in possession always seeks to prove himself to others by 'deeds or feats'. Look at me, look at me, look what I'm doing for humanity, that sort of thing. When you are in their presence, ask yourself: Do you feel good around them? Does the light shine through them? Do they seek to empower? Or does it feel like they only want power? Listen carefully to the words that come out of their mouths and watch their actions. When one speaks the truth and is living it, you will know. It is that simple," Margaret emphasized.

"So what do you do if you come across such a person?"

"You do nothing. You do not need what they have, be it a crystal skull or whatever sacred object you are connected to. It is there for you to tap into. That is all you need. The physical object is only the manifestation of the knowledge within."

"But if that's the case, then why have a physical object if the wrong people are in possession of it?" I asked again.

"There are many, many reasons depending on the karma of the people involved. It is not such a simple matter. There are many lessons to be learned from this. When people finally accept that there are sacred objects in the first place, they will be able to discern between a guardian and an owner. This then will enable them to work towards honoring those guardians and allowing them the access and exposure needed to work with these sacred objects," Margaret said.

"Going out there looking for 'treasure' is really a male thing," Mia interjected. "But you see, you can't truly possess a sacred object. Going after the deep meaning and working with the energy of it, is the female way and, as a guardian, it means keeping the energy alive."

Margaret continued, "All these things that come into our lives – the physical manifestation, whether it's an ancient Egyptian amulet or the Shroud of Turin - all they can ever do is remind us of the meaning which lies behind them. The objects themselves are not as important. What is important is the *essence* of what they are. People want the glory and the power of owning sacred objects without understanding what it really means to work with the objects' power. It's like Gollum in *Lord of the Rings* who wanted to possess the ring and, of course, it destroyed him. All possessing it did was to magnify his own darkness and he became weaker and weaker until he was overpowered. In the end, he not only lost the ring but he died from trying to get it back."

"Power and possession corrupts," Mia spoke softly but her voice carried. "The crystal skulls have the power to reveal your weaknesses and your strengths. That is why it's so important to be in your strength to face what you need to see, accept your deficiencies and let go of all that you no longer need. You can only go so far unless you are pure of heart. You may think that you are, you may believe that you are, weaving your own story for personal gain – but you cannot hide from us. So don't bother trying to use the skulls for ill. They will reflect the arrow you have drawn back onto you. You may not notice it at first, but the arrow will be drawn when you least expect it. Your ego can only grow so big, you will fall and fall you shall. For that is the law."

Her voice had changed. She carried a power and a depth that I had suspected but never witnessed until this moment. I knew that it was no longer Mia but the priestess who spoke. And I also knew that the warning was not only for me but for all those who sought its power for their own personal agenda. As I looked at Mia, I could imagine the garland of skulls around her neck - both the light and dark aspects protecting and keeping her in balance. I shivered all the same.

The priestess, as the embodiment of the skull itself, spoke once more:

"I am known by many names. The knowledge, the power and the beauty of Isis, Kali and the Great Mother Gaea: all these things I am, for I am the black skull. My domain is deep in the bowels of the earth, where the darkness lies. All things dark I am, but I am also of the light - the light that is contained within the darkness of creation. I am the counterpart of the light skull. My light is a different light. It is a denser vibration because it is black. Nevertheless, I contain all the colors of the rainbow. The light skull reflects light like a prism - rainbow colors shining brightly - but I do the reverse. I, the black skull draw the rainbow lights to me and absorb.

The veil is lifting; this is why I am being made known to you in this way. There is a need for the work that I do. There is a need for the darkness that no longer serves you to be removed so that a new dawning of light can emerge within you. But in order to be filled, you must first let go.

I am not for the faint of heart. Do not misunderstand this. Darkness comes in many forms and in many guises. If you are not humble, then you will be consumed, little by little, piece by piece - the arrogance reflected back onto yourself. The big Self will watch and lament in sorrow for the opportunity lost. So don't come looking for me if you are not prepared to see things as they are. But if you are ready, walk down the black spiral staircase. Slowly remove layer after layer of all things that you are not — as if you are taking off your clothes, piece by piece — mask upon mask that you have caked and stuck together with mud icing so that when you stand before me naked, you are not ashamed. I will see you as you are. And I will assist in eliminating all that you are not — those things of which you are not aware that have hung on for centuries, pulling you down like chain-mail making it difficult to move and to breathe.

If you are deep in despair, come and sit with me — unburden yourself. In the darkness, you have the time to reflect, to let go and to just be. And when you have deflated, a seed will sprout forth carrying with it the power of the creative, birthing new life to new ways of seeing and being.

Like the phoenix that consumes itself in fire — allow for me to consume your darkness. Feel the heat drawing closer — can you smell the scent of death? There is nothing like that smell. Even if you have never smelt it, you know it so well. And when the smell has gone, you will be free. Close your eyes so that they do not burn and allow yourself to see. The vultures will pick you clean so that nothing is left but your skeletal self — shining naked and white and crystal clear.

Dream yourself to be all that you are. Dream the power of your ancestry and call it forth. Dream yourself awake."

❧

We sat in silence for a good long while after that. I rolled another cigarette and watched the glowing embers and I breathed in the smoke. When you are in the presence of greatness, you know it. I was honored to be spoken to by the black skull. Up until that moment, I never even knew of its existence but of course it made sense. If there is a light skull – clear quartz – then so must there be a black skull and I imagined it to be black like obsidian.

For the first time, I understood what true power is all about and what it means to be powerful. Power doesn't take, it beats to its own steady rhythm, needing nothing and asking for nothing. When you meet it and accept it, then you are graced with empowerment which it gives off almost like an afterthought.

CHAPTER EIGHT

I could feel something happening before the event of that night. I hadn't known what it was but I had sensed it and it had been building all day. There was a quality in the air that had nothing to do with the incense that was burning in Margaret's living room. It was Japanese incense made by craftsmen specializing in invoking particular states of consciousness – incense of exceptional quality and refinement made of aloeswood and sandalwood blended to perfection. I had not known that such refinement existed and I marveled that such a scent could take me into a place of depth and stillness.

In the midst of our conversation, Margaret had sensed that the black skull wished to speak through Mia. She had gently lifted Ajax off her lap and onto his bed near the fireplace. On the mantelpiece was the incense. She lit it and waved it in the air a few times before sitting back down and making herself comfortable once again. There was only a faint trail of smoke that curled and danced its way above our heads but I watched and followed it and somewhere along the way as the smoke faded I closed my eyes and breathed in deeply. The smell of the incense seemed to be leading me down the black spiral staircase; to follow what the black skull was transmitting. And when

I reached her domain I was transported to another time and place. I knew it because the air was so clean and pure. It reminded me of what it must have been like millions of years ago before there were people on the planet - when the earth was new.

I found myself standing naked before her in her domain which was not easy at first. But there is something so liberating about nakedness. Imagine being two years old again; you are walking naked on the beach with the sun on your back as you toddle on your way to the sea. You are completely unaware that you are even naked. You are simply in a state of being. That is what it felt like to me. I was aware that I was naked but it did not seem to matter, there was no shame. If felt natural.

It takes time to allow yourself to unfold, unravel and unwind all the layers that have guarded you to the core. This process happens little by little until you find one day that you are so much more than you were. On that day, in the domain of the black skull, I felt something stir inside of me, as if another layer had come off. It was hard to let go of at first, but when I finally relaxed, I breathed such a sigh of relief to finally let go of the things that lay hidden and unnamed in the shadows of my psyche. I had been taken out of myself and transported into my true self. My mind became clearer as fresh energy flowed into the space where once this pain had been. It felt as if every single cell in my body had opened to receive this new energy which flowed like warm honey. My heart was wide open and I breathed a sigh of exquisite relief.

By now, I was back in my room at the Blue Diamond. I was glad in a way for this time alone because there was so much to integrate. This experience showed me how much I had longed for a magical life and now a door had opened up inside of me which would make that possible. More than anything, I wanted to be of service. And so I lay there with pillows propped up listening to the seagulls as I played out the various events of the last few days. I also took Margaret's words to heart - that Mia and I needed time to get used to being in each other's company. This was a relationship unlike any other - I had no reference. And as much as I longed to hold Mia in my arms I knew Margaret had been right.

❧

The next evening I took Mia to the Indian restaurant for what would be our last meal together for several weeks. I walked with my hands in my pockets and Mia slipped her arm around mine and drew me closer. We walked in silence, arm in arm, until we reached the restaurant.

The ambience was perfect. The other customers seemed to share our mood of quiet and relaxation. We had a table for four all to ourselves and I had ordered enough food for four. I was about to order wine but Mia, stopped me.

"Eliot, would you mind if we didn't have wine?" The waiter was standing beside me and was waiting for my order. I looked at Mia and knew that she did not want to discuss this in front of him so I simply ordered mineral water. When he had gone, Mia explained.

"I'd like to do so some more work with the skulls tonight. I would really like to show you how I formally call the skulls to me when I want their guidance and support. I get the feeling that it's time for us to start uncovering our connection. It's not good to have alcohol while working with the skulls, it would prevent us from keeping the lines of communication clear. Are you okay with that?"

Mia reached across the table and held my hand. I looked at her and nodded.

"I'd love to, Mia. I guess I have to get used to the fact that you're not a typical date! I'm excited, though."

"Glad I keep you on your toes," she said. "And eat up, I'd like you nice and grounded."

That part wasn't hard to do. Our meal was delicious. I ate like a king and felt like one. And while we were having our chai teas the conversation turned to the evening at hand.

"You know, Mia, it's strange because I know you so well in some ways and not at all in others. There is this ease that I feel with you. I know you can read my energy and through that, my thoughts – thankfully, not all of them but pretty much the gist of what I'm feeling and thinking." I could feel my face color.

She looked at me cocking her head in amusement. She was about to say something but sipped her tea instead and motioned for me to continue.

"I can feel it in your energy and I can see it. It's like when I'm with you, I feel this communication going on

at levels I'm not even aware of but I know it's happening. It's quite remarkable. This is all so new to me but I
am starting to become aware of this now. Usually, when
you meet someone you get to know them by starting from
the outside and slowly working your way in, if you're lucky.
But with you, from the first time we spoke at the museum,
even though we were conversing the way people do when
they've first met; it was totally different. We were connecting from the inside out."

"That's true," Mia said. "Which is why it was hard for
me to call you when you withdrew because even though we
hadn't discussed any of this, how could I phone you? You
would have run to the Himalayas and hidden in a cave."

"Most probably." I said, laughing at her joke.

"Small talk doesn't work with us." She said.

"I can truly see you as a priestess – such an un-
contemporary concept. Yet with you, it feels ancient and
modern at the same time and there is grace in that. Truly,
I am in awe at how you tap into our deepest mysteries so
easily and spontaneously. If someone were to meet you
though, they wouldn't have a clue that you can commune
with things that belong to another world. It's as if you
come alive in the darkness and shed light on that which is
hidden. Like what the black skull was saying…although I
have wondered how you can have these experiences and
also live with the mundane."

I didn't give her time to answer. I had more to say.

"After the black skull came through last night, I was
amazed. I felt so in the moment with what was going on.

I felt alive, vibrant, as if I had been privileged to be a witness, to be in on a secret that not many know about. I felt honored, special and so grateful. But then, after that experience, I found this sadness creep over me. You still have to get up the next day and pick up your life where you left it before you entered into the realm of mystery and magic. That extraordinary experience doesn't last. I don't mean that the healing didn't take place or the memory of it isn't there. It's just that state of being so open was gone and I wanted to go back there."

"I can't tell you how often I have thought of this myself," she said. "That is the scariest place really because you start to doubt – did I really experience what I thought I did? But the more you let go of your doubts, the more you can relax and live in the moment, accepting that you are living in two worlds that really are one. It's just that we are in a physical body. We do have to earn a living. Most of us aren't given the opportunity to just travel and study this stuff without having to lead another 'normal' life that pays the bills. And even so, even if it were easier, it's still challenging."

"So, do you think that opening yourself up to this knowledge means that you're going to become rich?" I was joking but was curious as to what she would say.

"No, not in the monetary sense." She said laughing. "But you can become abundant – abundant in the way that is correct for you. Not everyone needs a million pounds or dollars to live life to its fullest. In fact, the majority of us don't. It really doesn't have a whole lot to do with money anyway, rather, what you do with what you have. Like I was telling you that day when we were walking to Land's End - about what I think of the people down here, how we can all create and share abundance in so many different ways. There is no formula for success. It is all so personal. It does take a lot of courage to follow your path and your dreams. And when you do, a synchronicity starts to happen. You meet the right people at the right time; you are in the right place at the right time. Things start to fall into place although there didn't seem to be any logic to them. We might think something magical has happened to us but really, the opportunity, or chance, was always there waiting to be noticed. When we take that first step, then life takes on a different quality. When you believe in yourself, Eliot, then everyone and everything will as well. I really think so much of our frustration and sadness comes from not believing in our dreams. For me, having the skulls in my life is a reminder that all is not as it seems. We can't possibly know what our future holds but we can live in the faith that we will be taken care of in a way that is for our highest good. I bring myself back to that over and over again. Yet, after all these years, I too can feel sadness after a powerful evening such as we experienced."

"Are you saying that we have to persevere?"

"Persevere," she sighed. "There is something about that word – makes me think of struggle. And there's nothing like that feeling of overcoming an obstacle. You arrive at the finish line and realize that there was grace in all of that perseverance. For me, working and studying with people like Margaret, meditation, reading books that touch me deeply, yoga and listening to music all help me stay the course. Really, it's whatever works for you that will bring you to that place of peace inside. I don't think there's any one set way to keep emotionally and spiritually clear. Does that help at all?" she asked.

"Just listening to you has helped. And I feel it is something that I will need to hear over and over again."

"I know," was all she said for a while.

I wanted to ask her more about herself – to fill in the details of her life with timeframes – but there was nothing about Mia that allowed me to compartmentalize her in that way. Getting to know someone takes time. Intimacy, after all, is an honor. What she shared with me was what I needed to hear most – that she had been where I found myself now. We were more alike than I had realized.

⚜

After dinner we walked arm in arm along the promenade. The sea was pretty quiet with only gentle waves washing up to the shore. We wanted to go for a stroll before heading back to her place. We went as far as Battery Rocks then crossed the road walking past the Yacht Inn and up the steps into St Mary's churchyard. It was quite dark so we couldn't really see the gravestones, but it was nice to just walk around them.

"When I was a little girl, I had a babysitter who used to take me for walks in the cemetery along with her little dog.

Not once did she take me to a park. I wonder why that was, but I've so enjoyed walking in graveyards ever since. She was a bit like Margaret, come to think of it."

"Perhaps that was a way for you to not be afraid of such things like the dark and graveyards."

By now we had turned left onto Chapel Street and were heading back to Mia's place.

"I never thought of that! Thank you, Eliot. That makes a lot of sense."

"Glad to be of service, m'lady."

I bowed and she clapped her hands in delight. We don't bow to women anymore and that, I felt, was a pity. The gesture brought back the memory of an age where chivalry and honor were a rite of passage for men like me, and I reveled in the moment.

☙

Mia's house was inviting. It felt as if the house had wrapped its arms around me and embraced me in welcome. She gestured for me to go and make myself comfortable which I did. I sat back on the sofa watching her as she prepared the room for our session. She did not want me to help. I was glad of that simply because I so enjoyed watching her as she lit the candles and the incense. The fragrance of the Japanese incense was both grounding and exotic. It was the same scent, I noticed, Margaret had used in her home.

When all was done, Mia sat in her armchair. She wanted us to sit opposite rather than next to one another to provide enough distance between us. She said she liked being able to observe me and all that would pass between us. Tonight she had on a deep purple, flowing, long dress which seemed to enhance her role as a priestess. Whether this was intentional, or not, I do not know but I sat there waiting in anticipation for what was to come.

"Your imagination is the tool for accessing other states of consciousness and dimensions. This is what is meant by creative visualization or creative imagination. It is through your imagination that the doorway to other realms is opened and made accessible," Mia began.

"What you're saying is that by imagining you are in a specific place and time, you can actually go there?" I asked, somewhat incredulously.

"Yes, but there's more to it than that. Imagine you're listening to a radio show or a book on tape. You're just lying in bed being read to. As you are listening, you are transported right into the story. You can feel the adventure of the hero, his fears and his joys. You can feel the earth beneath your feet – all the descriptive narrative. You may even get so into the story that not only do you relate to the character, you become him. That's creative imagination."

"Oh, I see. So it doesn't matter that someone is doing the reading for you?"

"No, it doesn't matter at all. We visualize things all the time. You know the saying, 'our thoughts create our reality'?"

"Yes, I do. I've heard that a lot recently but there's something about it that just doesn't sit quite right with me. Try telling that to someone who's just lost their loved one."

"I understand what you're implying. There are some things that we can't change no matter how hard we try, things that we have no control over. There will always be hardship – that's part of being human – but we can choose how we deal with it and what we want to focus on," Mia said.

"I guess I just find it offensive if I'm struggling with something, to have someone come up and tell me that I have created it."

"Of course you would, Eliot, that's called insensitivity. Believe me; I've met a few people like that. But again, it's about discernment, and a lot of people like to judge, to blame. It's easier for someone to tell you that it's your fault that you're sick and walk away and do nothing, than to actually have the compassion to be with you no matter what the circumstances are."

"When you imagine that you are in a particular place and time, your energy shifts to accommodate the experience. Think about when you've had a nightmare, you wake up in a sweat with your heart pounding. It was so real that your body responded. When you start to see yourself in a particular situation, you can make your body believe that it is there. If matter is energy, then what we think about has energy too and this as we know has been proven to be so.

So, you can use creative imagination in a number of ways. One way is by doing ritual. Creating a sacred space, an altar dedicated to the energy that you wish to invoke within yourself or by evoking the energies of those beings that can guide you and assist you like the crystal skulls. Do you understand this, Eliot?"

"I think so. I'm just trying to follow, but please go easy with me. I need to take this slowly. I'm sorry."

"No problem," Mia said. "Sacred space enhances the mood and creates a place that is comfortable, safe and pleasant for you to delve into your own psyche. You always have to start with yourself. You can't expect to create magic when you are focused outside of yourself. So getting back to you listening to the story on the radio…In that moment you weren't focused on anything else, on acquiring anything. You were simply in the moment, and it is that moment that transported you into the story. That was all that mattered. Your whole being was in alignment with the story so that you could become part of it."

"That's a great analogy. I think what you're trying to say, Mia, is that since we are so used to being able to do that, we can also create an environment to enhance and evoke what we want to focus on. It's like working with the skulls to take us to the situation we wish to address."

"Exactly. We're just not used to thinking that we can affect change in this way. We think we're only daydreaming or using this tool," Mia paused and pointed to her head, "our great mind, for entertainment, when in fact, we can make an ally of our mind, make it work for us instead of allowing it to rule."

"I understand. I guess I never looked at it that way. I think of the mind as something that we use to think logically – to process things and give us answers in a step-by-step kind of a way, even if it's unconscious. My concern is that my mind always gets in the way. How could someone like me possibly meditate? I have no idea what it means to still the mind. My mind has never taken a rest willingly – only when I am completely taken off guard it seems. So by listening to a story, that's a way of taking my mind away from one thought and into another experience?"

"Yes, and that's exactly how I work with the skulls. I take you through a guided meditation so that you have something to focus on. From there it's up to you and that mind of yours."

She smiled at me then and we looked at each other for a long while. I don't know who shifted their gaze away first but it was Mia who spoke. "What is it that you would like to focus on this evening, Eliot?"

"I want to go back to Atlantis, to the connection that I know was so profound between us. Something happened back then. That much I do know, and I want some answers," I replied, surprised at my own resolve.

Mia had her eyes closed, listening to every word I said. I could tell that she was already communicating with the skulls. I was amazed at just how quickly she could change from being herself to being a priestess. I hadn't noticed but she had slipped on her ring, her 'special ring' as she called it, that she would only use for evoking the energy of the crystal skulls. It was a round, gold filigree ring with thirteen deep red garnet stones. An unusual ring, really. It was a big ring, and I remember thinking how small her hands were. Then my thoughts fell in with her words.

"I, Mia, call on the ancient crystal skulls to come and be with Eliot and myself."

Her voice held a depth that was not normally present. The air also changed becoming new and fresh.

"Know that you are shielded and protected by the ancient crystal skulls as you are by your other guides."

I closed my eyes and breathed in deeply as the priestess directed.

"Allow for your mind and body to open to receive."

I sat there waiting, expecting nothing, merely allowing myself to be guided.

"Imagine that you are sitting in the center of a circle with all the ancient crystal skulls around you. Guiding and supporting you on this journey into crystal consciousness."

It didn't take long; I was in another place and time – crystal time. Sitting there in the center of the circle, I was aware of the energies around me. It was easy to imagine it.

And then Mia spoke their words.

We have existed for a very long time but we come not from your past but from your future. We were placed back in time into your ancient past. This is possible because we exist beyond time, in what we call crystal time. You have not reached the level of awareness where you can successfully time travel as a race - although there are a few who know how to do this. But this is not common knowledge.

Time, as you know, is not linear although you experience it as such. It is more difficult to traverse the future time line than the past because your molecular structure in the future is much more highly advanced. The past, therefore, is more familiar to you as your physical body is more in alignment with it. The ancient crystal skulls can take you beyond time and into crystal time - the past and the present and the future connected and tied together, spiraling and circling around each other. When the proper alignment occurs within yourself, then it is possible to glimpse your past or your future.

When you journey into crystal time, much can be revealed to you. The knowing may happen on different levels. You may not always be conscious of all that is happening when working with the skulls, but your spirit knows and will carry this forward into your future. Your cells also know and will regenerate with this new awareness. In this way, you are developing your future DNA.

The light skull and the black skull are the master skulls. They embody all of the crystal skulls within them, as they contain all of the colors of the rainbow. If you can imagine the light skull as all that is above ground — conscious, accessible and illuminating — then the black skull is all that is beneath the surface of our consciousness. It rests at the bottom and can be likened to that of a guardian — a guardian of secrets of all that is hidden in the depths of your soul.

There are times when one needs the power of both the skulls in order to access particular states in consciousness. It's like two faces of the Divine evoked in harmony — the light skull, illuminating from the outside in, the black skull, illuminating from the inside out.

Mia paused and took a sip of water. I knew that when she spoke of the light skull, she was referring to the skull in my museum.

"Breathe in deeply and exhale slowly, Eliot, and begin to feel the base of your skull opening. The light skull will transmit her energy to you in that place. The base of your skull is designed for accessing ancient memories. So breathe in deeply."

I did as I was instructed. A white light that sometimes would turn into a golden color, flowed down my spine and, even though it came in through the base of my skull, it felt as if it were being poured over me. These sensations are so complex. You open yourself up to such another way of seeing and feeling that things happen all at the same time, just as when you are in the Dreamtime.

Mia continued. "Feel the light moving throughout your skeletal system. There is information encoded in the bones as there is information encoded on every level of your being. The bones, having density, can contain this energy. So feel it right down into your bone marrow. As you tune into this vibration, you will begin to notice just how powerful it is. Allow for the cells of your body to be encoded with this crystalline energy."

That was easy. Every single cell in my body was open, receiving this attunement. A long time seemed to have passed before I heard her speak again.

"Now place the skull on top of your own skull, as if you are wearing a mask."

Oh, how wonderful, I thought, and how easy.

"From this place all is possible. Allow yourself to move beyond time and space to where you need to go – to where we need to go. I am here with you, Eliot. I am journeying *with* you."

It wasn't like I felt myself land somewhere. It was more like someone had drawn the curtains and I was looking out through a window at Mia on the other side of the glass. She couldn't see me. She looked different but the same. I can't explain why that is. It's like what you've experienced in dreams. You dream about a person you know but in the dream, they look completely different. Yet you know that it is that person – I guess it's the essence of familiarity you sense. However, it wasn't just her essence. I could actually smell her fragrance, as well. It was, and still, is a mixture of sandalwood, amber and neroli. She had long red hair, much like her hair is today, but much longer. It was almost as long as she was tall which gave her the appearance of being smaller than she actually was – and we were a tall race. She wore a tunic and flowing trousers. They could have been clothes that she would actually wear now, loose fitting and comfortable.

I can't tell you the year, only that it was the time when Atlantis was nearing its end. The pyramids had not yet been built but the Sphinx, which is much older, had been. We were living far away from Egypt. Atlantis was a big continent, almost twice as large as North America and we lived in the north which then had a southern climate. All this I knew in an instant.

I met Mia then at a very young age – six years old. There were several classes that both boys and girls would attend together. And there was an instant connection between us; I guess you could say I recognized her even then. We were taught the subject of reincarnation so I just accepted the fact that we had known each other before. It wasn't such a big deal. It's just how it was.

After playing, we were asked to form two lines, one for the boys and one for the girls. We were going our separate ways. But I left my queue and stood behind Mia. It was her hair that enthralled me and I wanted to smell it. Out of all of the senses, my sense of smell seems to have a life of its own. It is still that way to this day. It tells me things. If I don't like the smell of some food, I don't eat it. If I don't like the smell of someone, I don't do business with them. And smelling beautiful fragrances has always been pleasurable.

When the teacher pulled me out of the line and scolded me, the boys made fun of me and the girls giggled. But Mia's eyes followed mine, letting me know that all was well with us.

Not everything about Atlantis was as wonderful as some would expect you to believe. There were periods of strife and hardship. Just because a society is technologically advanced does not mean that its residents are the spiritual equivalent. So then as now there existed many kinds of people occupying the same space but almost in different dimensions. The scene had shifted and I was now an adult. I was a scientist and I had access to certain instruments that were considered very dangerous, the equivalent of today's nuclear technology. In order to become a scientist, you also had to be a magician in the sense that your training was not only in the scientific arena, but also of the mysteries. We were taught in what was known as the Mystery Schools. We learned to control our thoughts for focus and concentration and thought transference, telepathy. And as we became more adept, we also learned how to control the forces of nature. Our minds were highly developed. However, intellect is not the same as power. Intellectual knowledge may bring about power, but intellect for its own sake, is not balanced and wreaks as much havoc as a heart without a head. The people I became associated with were of this intellectual type and I grew increasingly like them. We were visionaries who had become blinded by intellectual dogma. The writing was on the wall. Atlantis had become so out of balance it would fall but my group did not believe it. We thought we had the power to control that which is un-named and irrepressible.

What started as one truth became many, as the Mystery Schools branched out into particular specialties, losing sight of the fact that they had evolved from the same teachings. An imbalance grew but the distortion of the teachings had happened long before I entered into my field.

I don't quite know when the split occurred between the two major factions. I guess I didn't really want to know – ignorance, or worse, complacency, comes to mind.

The first group was known as the Light of Light and the other, the Sons of Truth. The latter was originally known as The Sons and Daughters of Truth but the Sons took over and, as the name suggests, they were patriarchal in nature. The truth part of their name, however, was far from ac-curate. In the beginning, their stance was to seek the truth through scientific inquiry, and for a long time, they were ingenious in their discoveries. Technological advancement prevailed and enabled Atlantis to thrive and be the greatest civilization that ever lived. By the time I got involved with them however, the Sons of Truth were only a fragment of what they once were. And most, myself included, did not notice when corruption and greed sprouted and took root which grew so thick and tangled that they choked the very essence of life itself – not until it was too late.

My name was Ariam which means 'seeker of knowledge.' I looked pretty much the same as I do now, only a bit taller. Our foreheads were slightly elongated, a sign of nobility and intelligence. The ancient Egyptians carried this trait as well. But over time, that particular gene became dormant within our DNA, waiting for the proper alignment to once again reawaken.

I speak to you both as Ariam and as Eliot, so please have patience in the recounting of this tale. In essence, we are one and the same. I, Ariam, in the last days of life looked into the crystal of the future, enabling me to see what lay before me – asking of it when, in time, I could make amends.

Just as we have individual karma to work through so, too, is there collective karma. Each generation, each century and each civilization have their own particular karma. Many of those incarnated now were inhabitants of Atlantis. The source, then, of the narrow, fundamental beliefs in your time stem from there. Many do not have the understanding or ability to seek beyond their comfort zone. However, because of your understanding of this, a healing will naturally begin to occur. The people of Eliot's time are inadvertently do-ing much the same as our scientists did, although it emerges from a completely different strand of the same pattern of consciousness. That is, to believe in a particular brand of truth, one must overlook the havoc wrought by denying those in disagreement, their right to personal freedom.

For example, in your present day, stem cell research is on an upswing. There are those opposed to this for religious purposes and the like. What they carry is the fear and the remembrance of what happened with the experimentation of our day. Stem cell research, as you call it now, is not in and of itself harmful to life but rather an enhancement. However, it is, in a sense, where the downfall of Atlantis occurred. At first, the research and subsequent discovery enhanced medicine and healing on many levels. But as scientists became more locked into their own universe, competing against each other for recognition and status, experiments became more bold and impetuous so that people, especially women, were reduced to the status of human guinea pigs. The children they bore were different.

Some scientists wanted to create a new race, a race of hard-working, beast-like humans who would thrive on manual labor and follow direction without question. However, other scientists wanted to manipulate DNA so that the right hemisphere of the brain would be more developed. They did this in order to create those that would be reared as human oracles. The Sons of Truth, having overdeveloped the logical side of their brains; had lost their intuitive, nurturing side and, consequently, their ability to communicate telepathically.

Children began to be born that were unusual. Some looked the same but their auras, their energy fields, were so very different. It was something that you felt instantly, which caused people to reject and even abandon these children.

Imagine meeting an alien from outer space cloaked in a human body. They may look the same but you know that there's something that's just not quite right. It was like that. Our senses were sharper then and, even in your present day, you would be able to notice this. It was the same with their eyes. There was something behind those eyes that would make you want to turn away, to not look straight at them for these children possessed the ability to look right inside of you. Nothing in a sense was hidden from them but they, being children, did not know how to mask this. They had the ability to show you your deepest fears. When you looked into their eyes, you would see your own disillusionment and fear reflected. What most did not realize, was that if you faced your fears, they would also show you your greatest gifts.

As with any child when they are not properly nurtured and cared for, the very core of their being becomes fundamentally damaged. They carried a depth of sadness that one can only imagine. To be rejected, not only by your own flesh, but also by society as a whole, was unbearable and cruel. The children of whom I speak were those genetically manipulated to act as oracles. They carried an acute sensitivity so that harsh words, or a harsh environment, were difficult for them to adjust to. Some of these children developed sensitivity in their hands and needed to be gloved with thick leather. These experiments went on far too long.

Research is fundamental to the development of any civilization. However, there is a difference between research and experimentation. I can't help but liken this Atlantean experience to the experimentation carried on by the Nazis of your own era. Although ours was more 'humane', suffering was prevalent and that, in and of itself, was dreadful. The destruction of Atlantis had to happen because there was no other way to destroy the collective unconscious ego. It wasn't that someone flipped a switch and the catastrophe began like some nuclear explosion. It was so much more complex. It began with those that thought they could play God, mistakenly thinking that God and Ego are one and the same. The consequences you know about. It created a tilting of the earth's axis. South became north and north became south. All perished that remained.

I would now like to relay Mia's story as it was revealed to us that night.

"Even in Atlantis there were many who did not know of the existence of the ancient crystal skulls although crystal technology prevailed. The Sons, however, sought to use the skulls for their own purposes. The black skull had been hidden long before and sent by some of the guardians to a place unknown by many in our day. The black skull's gift is to access the divine feminine nature. This skull was revered centuries before but when the Sons took power, the energy of the black skull was no longer accepted nor needed in the same way, so it was removed to a place where the energy could rest deep in the bowels of the earth.

They say that time heals all wounds. I, Mia, have blocked out the memory of this place for a long time. It pains me to think that I thought that was the only way. All that sadness and pain that I experienced in my regression led me to lives and pathways I would not have consciously chosen. I believe we all have experienced that in some fashion. I guess you could say I took that so literally that I waited centuries to find my way back. But a piece of light shone through the darkness. I sought that light, lifetime after lifetime, until it grew, enveloped and nourished me once again, as in the days of old.

My name was O'Saragh. The O is silent and may be likened to the meaning of the Ouroboros, a symbol of regeneration and unity. I was part of a group known as the Light of Light, living and working in a place known as the Temple of Light. The Temple was an incredible place. Nothing in your present day exists that is like it although many dream of this place and long to recreate it. We had a community of people with the same vision, to keep the tradition of healing and mystery alive. The temple was a large structure spanning several acres. We grew most of our own produce and were self-sufficient in almost all aspects so we took in all those special children, and all those people that needed help and taught them how to honor and live with their uniqueness. All were welcome.

The final days were truly desperate. Many guardians left to safeguard the skulls and the teachings. The light skull had made many journeys before reaching the Americas where it was rediscovered. I chose to stay to help those transitioning from this life in Atlantis back to Source. I was already in contact with those on the other side; waiting to guide us through the process we call death. Even with all of my knowing - my connection and communication with beings beyond this plane - I was afraid. But I did my best not to show it. I had to stand tall for those that needed my support and guidance. Many people came to the temple as a last resort seeking comfort and answers. I did not hide the truth. The more awakened we could become upon our time of death, the easier the transition would be. And so I did my best, but fear is a strange thing. It nearly tore me apart - so many to guide while remaining a pillar of strength. It exhausted me. I dreamt of sleep every waking moment. I longed for sleep and, in a sense, that is what happened to me lifetime after lifetime.

Surrender and allow for divine will to guide you, I would chant over and over again in my waking state to all those that looked to me as a savior. But it was the children who understood and, not surprisingly, guided the adults towards this transition.

In those moments, many were given a gift because so many were perishing at the same time. The gift was to understand why and how the circumstances that led to this event took place and how in the future they could be of assistance. This created a healing that reverberated throughout the cosmos. A pledge was made to reincarnate once again when such a time may arise. In our present day, there has never been anything like the pollution and destruction of our natural resources. Even the Sons understood the necessity of caring for the earth. This is why all those now fighting for the protection of our earth's resources: healers, visionaries, scientists, artists, mystics – they all speak from personal experience in order to make our world a better place.

∾ঌ

Ariam's Story

I ran as fast as I could, exhausted and out of breath to the Temple to be with O'Saragh. I pushed my way boldly across the throngs of people to reach her. The sky was a deep gray and the air smelled of sulfur. It wasn't that cold but the dampness made me feel as if it were. Standing there, looking at her made me shiver even though I had run miles. She trembled as well. I didn't want to look at her; the shame that I carried consumed and compressed me. But she leaned against me seeking comfort and I found a strength I didn't know I possessed. There was a depth of sadness and resignation as our eyes met.

"I am so sorry," I whispered.

"It's not your fault," O'Saragh said.

"Yes, in many ways, it is. I could have stopped them. I said nothing. I didn't want to believe."

"We must get back to the children," she replied.

It surprised me that O'Saragh could be so welcoming. When it came, it didn't last long – we stood on the roof, holding hands. I asked for forgiveness and prayed for redemption. The tsunami hit hard and fast.

∾ঌ

O'Saragh's Story

I knew when the tsunami would hit. I could feel the vibration rising hours before it happened. When I looked into Ariam's eyes, his life flashed before me like in one of your silent movies. In that moment I saw the perfection of it all and it gave me courage.

Silence, darkness, light – respite. That is all I remember."

❧

I heard Mia's voice calling me back.

"It is time to return to this current place and time. When you are ready open your eyes and tell me how you are."

I didn't have to tell her how I was, she already knew. The tears had been flowing down both of our faces. I knelt at her feet, my head resting on her lap and wept.

We waited a long while before we spoke again.

"I didn't realize that we could experience the same event at the same time. To both be the person that I am now and at the same time relive the person that I was then and speak from that voice." It's extraordinary." I said.

"It is extraordinary. I've never experienced anything like this either. But the right alignment occurred for this to happen for us. In order to understand and fulfill our destiny." Mia said.

"I guess you're right, Mia. It's a lot to take in."

We were both drained. I got up and made us hot drinks. We needed reviving. Mia was stretched on the floor like a cat when I returned with our teas. I went to lie down on the sofa and motioned for her to join me. We spoke in low voices even though no one could possibly hear us.

"Can you see why you felt as if you were carrying a burden?" Mia asked me.

"Yes," I replied. "It seems we hold onto the memory of a traumatic event through the emotion of how that felt. It stays with us and grows like boulders on our backs, lifetime after lifetime. We end up making the emotion be the most important memory and take that on as our cross to bear."

"But now that you have the understanding, you can finally let go, Eliot," Mia said looking up at me. "You weren't to blame. You, being of a transpersonal nature, felt responsible and carried that burden for all those that perpetrated the fall of Atlantis. Now that we are living in an age where humanity is at a crossroads, we can assist in educating and transforming consciousness so that we don't repeat the same mistakes. There are so many people out there like us, Eliot."

"*Exactly*, like us?" I asked, jokingly.

"Well, not quite but you know very well what I mean."

The shutters had not been drawn and I was thankful for it. I looked out of the window and could see the plants in the front garden. Strange, I thought, how I never noticed the large palm tree before. It's long, spiky leaves were almost touching the window pane, as though looking in on us, wondering at our strangeness as I was wondering the same about it. Peaceful and serene now, I was about to say something quite profound. I thought that the words were coming out of my mouth. It was beautiful what I was thinking and feeling but instead, I fell asleep right where I was on the sofa, in Mia's arms.

CHAPTER NINE

I hadn't been back at work more than a week when the skull was returned from the Institute. The results of the tests had been 'inconclusive'. I found it odd that they didn't share all of their findings but, to be honest, I wasn't that interested. I didn't need 'experts' to repudiate what I now knew to be the truth: this skull was the real deal. My focus was elsewhere.

For some reason, I had decided not to put the skull back on display and instead, left it in a locked cabinet in my office. I kept it inside an old black leather carrying case. The interior of the case was lined with thick black velvet cushioning that had been specially made for it a long time ago. Recently we had updated the skull's security casing but I had come across this old case a few years back and had kept it. I'm glad that I did because it was the perfect place for it until the time was right to put it back on display. For now it felt so right to have the skull nearby.

My office was situated at the back of the museum quite hidden from the public; near the side entrance on Montague Street, almost directly opposite where Mia used to stay. It appeared to be a pretty messy office, stacks of papers everywhere. But really there was order to my madness and I was lucky to have my own space as my colleague was on sabbatical. My desk, which was too large for the tiny room and made of oak, was placed in front of the window. I was lucky to have a decent desk and even luckier to have a window in the room. Many of the museum staff are housed below ground, having to contend with artificial light all day. The sun was streaming in and was right in my eyes this particular afternoon and as I reached to pull the blinds down it occurred to me that the skull would benefit from the natural sunlight.

I started to clear some stacks of paper using my absent colleague's desk and chair for some of my filing. Then I locked the door and took out the skull. I placed it on the windowsill at first but it felt too exposed to me there so I moved it onto my desk, where it was still in the sun. This soon became a regular habit of mine.

I was spending a lot more time at work, going in on the weekends when the regular office workers weren't there. I'd always lock the door although logically there would have been no need to. As an artifact the skull would have been under my jurisdiction and I frequently had some ancient piece or other on my desk. Maybe it was because I didn't want anyone bursting in on me while I was in the middle of talking to the skull. This I often did now. It felt completely natural to me, like talking to a good friend, but nothing extraordinary happened - no signs, or experiences of any kind. All I can say is that I got a lot of work done. And the more the skull bathed in the sunlight, the clearer and fresher and younger the air felt in my little office.

A few weekends went by like this and then, on the fourth weekend when it was time for me to place the skull back inside its case, I heard a voice in my head loud and clear. *Thank you*, was all it said. It startled me. Up until then it had been me who had been doing all the talking. But it was that voice that gave me the courage to proceed with what I did next. I took that case and walked right out of the museum in broad daylight. As I locked the door to my office, my heart was pounding and my shirt was sticking to my back. I felt incredibly hot but I walked along the corridor, down the steps and out of the entrance with such confidence and self-assurance that no one seemed to notice. It looked as if I was carrying an oversized briefcase. I think that even if the guards had noticed, I walked with such an air of normalcy and purpose that no one gave me a second glance or thought me odd. I felt both invisible and invincible.

For one whose mind rarely rests, my head, at this moment, was unusually quiet. In fact, it must have been deep in sleep resting on Morpheus' shoulder. It wasn't until I got home, took the skull out of its case and placed it on my dining room table that I realized the enormity of what I had done. Imagine taking the Mona Lisa home because you felt a 'connection' to it. Who would believe you and grant you clemency? The fear and apprehension of the consequences of my actions hit me. I wouldn't just lose my job; I would go to prison! So I did what any normal man would do under the circumstances, I poured myself a few shots of whisky. I practically gulped them down, coughing and spluttering as I nearly choked on the burning liquid. Pouring scotch into my favorite glass tumbler and adding a drop of water is a ritual I thoroughly enjoy. Today, there was none of that. This wasn't a drink, it was a lifeline. I even drank standing up. I leaned against the kitchen counter and reached for a tea towel to wipe the splutter off of my shirt. Then I went to double check that the front door was locked and bolted, and the backdoor as well as all the windows. In fact, I even searched the house for intruders. I started thinking that perhaps I really had gone mad. But then I looked in on the skull and I knew that I hadn't.

This was an extraordinary skull. It was completely clear with a detachable jaw and each tooth individually carved. It was a masterpiece, truly a work of art. The skull has prisms inside and the light from my Tiffany lamp was reflecting down onto it. My dining room is a room not often used, as I can't remember the last time I entertained. However, it was a room with a working fireplace and I actually made a fire in there to honor my guest.

It was Saturday evening. I had an old leather armchair which was situated in the corner with the Tiffany lamp next to it and there I sat all evening. It was a hodgepodge of a room - antique furniture, paintings and what not. I watched the skull from this place as it glowed and sparkled with colors I had never seen before reflecting, sparkling and dancing to life. The fear and anxiety that I had felt soon melted away. I was mesmerized.

I could not take my eyes off it. I even ate my dinner, leftover curry from a takeaway I had the night before, in that armchair. I wanted a clear head and remembered Mia's words about not drinking. Considering the state I had been in, the whisky I'd drunk earlier had worn off by now and I felt I wasn't inebriated in any way. But now I was relaxed with a cup of coffee in hand. The skull needed light and air and 'company' from someone who recognized it and treasured it, not for its monetary value but rather for what it truly was – a tool for transformation. I dared not tell anyone of my tryst, especially Mia – not yet anyway. I hadn't even mentioned that the skull was back from the Natural History Institute.

Later, I retired into my bedroom, carefully carrying the skull up the stairs. There was a candle on my bedside table and I placed the skull in front of it. I guess I was just experimenting with different lights and the effects it might have on the skull – and me. Usually I read before sleep but that evening, I just lay there half expecting something to happen, somehow. All I did was fall asleep.

I woke up in the middle of the night. Something was happening to me, something extraordinary. I had the sensation of energy running up and down my body, like an electrical current. I saw a myriad of pathways connecting and crossing through my energy centers. If you've ever seen a map of the human body with the acupuncture points or meridians, as they are known in traditional Chinese medicine, then you'll know what I'm referring to. This lasted for a while and it felt as if I was having an acupuncture treatment although I had never experienced one before. And then the microcosm grew into a macrocosm. I could see that there were energy lines all over the earth and beyond. Perhaps this is what they mean by ley lines, I thought.

We hear that saying all the time about how we are all connected and that the earth is a living organism. As I lay there in bed, I could see clearly that I was made up of energy. My body looked like a mandala connected to an ever expanding field of other mandalas spanning the entire earth, filled its belly and radiated out into space. We, all of humanity, all of life on this planet and all of the cosmos, formed the most beautiful patterns together.

There is something profound about making a connection such as this, suddenly gaining an understanding without going through the process of 'learning'. The thoughts somehow form in your mind, these abstract patterns lying there waiting for you to connect the dots. The skull was definitely transmitting something but it was up to me to be open to receive.

We are told that if we have 20/20 vision, we have perfect eyesight. But there is another type of vision that we can develop – the ability to see things from a different perspective. That is what enables us to become extraordinary human beings. When we no longer view the world from our own myopia but rather from a perspective so broad and infinite, anything is possible.

༄

Another week went by and I pretty much kept to myself. Mia and I spoke often but she was busy making and designing costumes for a theatre company and had a deadline much to my relief. This meant that sometimes a few evenings would go by without us communicating with each other. It wasn't that I was keeping secrets from her. In hindsight I think what I wanted was my own connection to convey to her. And I was waiting for the right timing to share my experiences. I wanted to please her, to show her that, for at least a little while, I could give the skull the freedom to simply be what it wanted to be in my home as opposed to some artifact locked up in a museum.

So I kept the skull in my bedroom. I felt it was safe there and, when I got home at night, I would carry it downstairs to the dining room and sit with it. I realized that you can't will something to happen, so my excuse would be that I was just keeping it company and allowing it to get fresh air and sunlight. But really what I wanted more than anything was to have another experience. I wanted to understand the mysteries of the universe without waiting for divine timing and the understanding that there is a process in all things. I had experienced and understood so much but I wanted more. I don't know why I was trying to push something that does not operate according to my own needs. I've heard Mia say often enough that we have to be in alignment; yet I had a feeling that I had something to prove. I suddenly recognized the essence of the Ego, that part of us that has no concept or understanding of Humility, Ego's brother and adversary. I already knew about my mind getting in the way of things and thought I had a handle on it. It's easy to forget that there are so many points of entry and distraction that take us away from our center.

I suppose I am only to blame for what followed:

I was sitting in my old leather armchair and imagined, (or perhaps I willed myself to imagine) I was in the center of the circle with all the ancient crystal skulls around me. I called the skulls to me out loud the way Mia had done and guided myself through the process, just as she had. I got up and sat at the dinner table and placed my hands on the skull. It was smooth and cold at first and I shivered briefly until I got used to the sensation.

I breathed in deeply and was still - so still that I found myself sitting in the center of the circle. I no longer had to imagine anything. I was in another place and time sitting cross-legged on the ground with all the skulls around me. We were at eye level with each other. It seemed as if they were sitting on podiums. I could feel the ones that were behind me, although I could not see them. The light skull was in the center. Not only was it physically in front of me, but it was also in front of me in this place in crystal time. I understood that I was in their residence, a desert-like place with no visual distractions. It made sense that there would be nothing there as all was inside of the skulls. I could feel them all wanting to speak to me. I felt elated. My attention would get drawn to one of the skulls and then to another and then another. I didn't know where to keep my focus because I knew that they all had so much to share. There was so much knowledge to tap into that I felt like a child in a candy store.

My breathing changed. I started inhaling and exhaling a lot quicker, making a lot of noise as I exhaled, almost like trying to blow out the excess of all this energy. Their combined vibrational energy was overwhelmingly powerful. Sitting there was very different from what I had experienced with Mia. That experience had been beautiful, this one was power magnified. Every single cell in my body was electrified and I was in awe. I focused on breathing more slowly and as I did, they spoke as one voice:

You have asked for knowledge, you have asked for power and you have asked for wisdom. However, in order to have these things you must first understand the dark as well as the light. To have true power is to be in balance. And so here is the dark.

I was standing on a cliff-top and all around me was darkness. Within the darkness, every atrocity imaginable was contained - beating, it seemed, to an unknown pulse. They gave me the blessing of detachment so that I could see, feel, and sense but not be affected by what I saw. Nevertheless, it was very disturbing. There was nothing to see. The pulsing of the dark was like a buzzing sound. I could feel what was within, what was being consumed. If I focused too long on one particular point, I knew that I could be drawn into that experience. What was contained was vast – an infinity of darkness. I remained an observer, detached, standing on the cliff-top, viewing the picture in its entirety. The moment I realized that the darkness and the dark forces that rule were being watched by me was the moment I sensed that I was all alone. The darkness pressed up against me, trying to envelop me, getting closer and closer. I knew I could not panic that I had to stay still and breathe. I had to remain calm. But fear was gripping me now. An oppression of thoughts started to eat away at me: *Who do you think you are? How dare you think that you can come here and observe us? How dare you think that you are special enough and powerful enough to not be affected by us?*

They were mocking and jeering at me. Was I just thinking these things because I was afraid and I thought that this is what scary disincarnate beings would say? Or was it truly the darkness trying to find its way in? The more they insulted me, the more afraid I became. I did not know how to hold my ground.

"You fool," I thought. "You stupid fool."

But it was no good beating myself up. I could see that there were plenty waiting for the opportunity to do just that. I called to the skulls but couldn't re-connect with them.

"Stay calm, Eliot, please just stay calm," I said to myself. I was in limbo, afloat in nothingness and I didn't know what to do. I breathed. I tried to think positive thoughts. I thought of Mia, calling to her to come and find me. But my mind kept getting in the way, pulling me back into my fear, despair, and utter loneliness.

"Mia, Mia, please help me." I tried to keep focusing on her energy, her strength, and imagined that she was there, guiding me back to safety. And so I continued, calling her name, focusing on her and knowing that the only way forward was to not give up.

I was no longer standing on the cliff top but instead, I had slipped and fallen. Holding on to a branch, I didn't seem to have the strength to pull myself back up to safety. Looking down at what lay beneath made me feel dizzy and all the more terrified. It looked like a whirlpool of black mass on top of an even darker mass of black.

The phone rang and I nearly jumped out of and then back into my skin at the same time. Trembling, I took my hands off the skull. I hadn't realized that I had had my hands on it the entire time. They felt cold and stiff. I must have been gripping the skull with all my strength because my fingers felt numb and it took a few seconds for me to reach into my pocket and pick up the phone. My eyes also had to adjust; my vision was blurred and I fumbled with the phone which fell and slid across the room. I swore every curse I knew and made up some new ones. I fell, twisting my leg in the process and banged my knee hard. I yelled out loud. It was the knee I had injured skiing and that had never been right since. The phone kept on ringing and I crawled for it on all fours.

I picked up the phone. It was Mia. I closed my eyes for the briefest moment and found myself back hanging on to that branch disconnected and frightened.

"Eliot, what's the matter with you?"

I was breathing hard. It took me a while to calm myself enough to be able to speak to her. Her energy on the other end of the line felt like a balm to me.

"I'm so glad you phoned. Please help me," I sobbed.

It was hard to breathe - the dark was pressing up against me.

"I was trying to work with the skulls, Mia, but I ended up in this dark place. I can't seem to get out of it," I said desperately. I could hear her breathe in sharply.

She spoke forcefully but calmly. "Just listen to my voice. Let me guide you. See yourself in the center of the circle with all the crystal skulls around you. You are not alone, Eliot. You were never alone. Claim your space, Eliot; command them to depart, away from you and out of your sight."

I had one hand on the phone, listening to Mia, and with the other, I held onto my heart. I was still on the floor but I managed to crawl to the corner and leaned against the wall. My heart was beating so fast, I thought I would have a heart attack right there and then, so I composed myself as best as I could and did as I was told. I could feel my strength and my power returning. It was that same power that I had felt earlier when I first went into the circle. But this time, I could contain it and it was that strength that carried me out of the darkness and back into the light.

"Never forget who you are, Eliot. Breathe into your heart and then push the energy down into your solar plexus. Feel your strength returning."

It was so good to hear her voice. My heart had stopped its erratic behavior and was now open and serene. I didn't have time to think about the consequences of my actions. I was just glad to be back. The skull was on the dining room table. It glowed in the light as it always did. I didn't feel any judgment; if anything, I felt the skull was glad I had made it through in one piece.

"Eliot, I'd like you to take a walk, really ground yourself. And when you are calm, call me back," Mia said.

It was raining, dark and gloomy. The last thing in the world I wanted to do was to be out in that rain, but I did as she suggested. My knee throbbed and my leg hurt but I went out in the rain, with raincoat and umbrella. I even donned my cap. I had prepared for the weather far better than I had for my earlier experience. Outside I found a long stick just lying only a few feet away from me. How it got there, I will never know but it was the perfect stick, thick and sturdy and I used it as a crutch. I walked a good long while around the heath where I live. The rain eased to a light drizzle and it was revitalizing. There is something powerful about walking and thinking, thinking and walking – enabling parts of your psyche to build a rhythm and come out and present itself clear and clean.

What I had experienced felt very much like a nightmare. I realized now that if I had been stronger, I could have stood my ground. Instead, I had panicked and taken refuge in my head yet again. Staying in the moment means to be really focused on the rhythm of your breath, feeling the life force within you sound and strong, knowing with all your heart you are protected and guided.

I realized two things: firstly, that I had wanted to impress Mia - that I had wanted her to see just how far I had come. How silly, really, because spiritual growth is not something that you can try and impress someone else with. It is yours; it is personal, between you and the Divine – no one else. The moment that you try to impress someone implies that you are not moving towards self-realization. You are focused on an outcome. For me, the outcome was about impressing a woman that meant a lot to me.

Secondly, I understood just how we can get caught up in the illusion of greatness. Just because we may have some form of authority does not mean that we can take what is not ours for the taking. I am not a guardian of the skull. That is usually a woman's role, has been for centuries and will continue to be for a long time to come. By what right did I have to take the skull home with me? I know all the reasons I had given myself before. I wanted to be of service but being of service means that you do not put yourself in the center. It means that you let go of your own needs to serve the highest good. That's the part I had lost sight of.

When I returned home, I called Mia as she had instructed. We did not speak for long, just enough for Mia to gauge whether I was truly all right or not. I was fine, if a little ashamed.

The next day was Saturday, which meant there would be few colleagues about the museum and I could take the skull back first thing. I felt a pang of regret as I locked it away in my office. It was as though in an instant the air around me had become stale again.

⚜

I drove like a fiend. I sent Mia a text to let her know when I would arrive. No apology for the previous night. No further explanation. I wanted to see her in person.

"You made it," she said as she opened the door to me. She held out her hand for my coat. I handed it to her without a word.

"It's so good to see you back in one piece." She squeezed me tightly to her.

"Please sit down, Eliot. I'll go and get you some tea."

"Thank you," I said, finally relaxing.

"I know just how much tea is the all-round drink for any occasion here in the UK," she called from the kitchen. "Good times, bad times, social times and challenging times," Mia said and returned with a tray. She handed me my cup. "So please, unwind and have your tea. You must be exhausted."

"I think we'll probably need quite a few more cups then," I said jokingly.

"Well, whatever it takes, Eliot. We have all weekend. You really did unnerve me, you know."

"I'm sorry. Truly, I am," I said. "And thank you so much for coming to my rescue. I was in such a state; I didn't even have time to ask you what happened for you in all of this - how you knew to call me just at that moment."

"I've known something was up for a while, just with you in general. But I got that you were okay – just processing and going through stuff. I didn't call sooner because the last few times we've spoken, you seemed a bit aloof. I knew that it had nothing to do with me because you told me how busy you've been with work. I just knew that you needed your space and thought it best not to intrude. I knew you would contact me when you were ready. I've never wanted you to feel any kind of pressure, Eliot. But then last night, I knew something was really wrong. I heard you actually calling my name. It was surreal. I could see that you were suspended in limbo, in a dark place and that what was happening was not an ordinary thing. If I hadn't been able to get through to you on the phone, I would have worked on you from a distance, telepathically letting you know that I was helping you."

I started to tell her everything starting from the time I placed the skull on the windowsill in my office. When I got to the part about taking it home, Mia interrupted.

"You did WHAT?" Mia shouted.

I was taken aback. I hadn't expected that sort of a reaction. There was so much going on that night that I had conveniently forgotten the most important part.

"What has gotten into you, Eliot?"

I could feel my large body crumple; trying to make myself small, which of course was not possible.

She got up and walked into the kitchen to get us more tea but really, I think it was because she wanted time to think about what she was going to say next.

"Please, let me explain," I said, when she returned. I did the best I could, leaving nothing out. All my revelations of wanting to please her, of the skull saying, thank you - all of it.

She was calmer then.

"Now you understand what I meant about working with power objects. You have to work within the laws, Eliot. And I'm not just talking about the laws of the country you happen to be in but spiritual laws. You have to be careful and really clear about what you are doing. Is it for the benefit of humankind or is it for your personal benefit? We have discussed this before."

"I know. I understand. But sometimes the laws of a nation are corrupt. Just think about a dictatorship - that law would not be in accordance with spiritual laws."

"Of course it wouldn't," Mia said patiently. "But again, it's about discernment. It's so easy to weave in your own personal story of why you want to do a particular thing - like take home the skull. Remember that the skulls magnify what you are thinking and feeling. They are a conduit of energy. It doesn't matter if your thoughts are good or bad — they're just going to amplify them. I noticed that a lot when I would visit the museum, when the skull was on display. People would come to see the skull for all sorts of reasons. I'm not talking about the ones who were just curious, wanting to see what's on exhibit, but the ones who had a sense that this skull is a sacred power object. I witnessed people bursting into tears at the sight of it, while others had the opposite reaction and would burst out laughing. Some wore expressions of awe and deep gratitude. Some were fearful. You name it, everything under the sun. But the ones who pretended to be one thing and were actually something different — they really stood out. I could see their big egos. Even you noticed that without knowing anything about this stuff."

"I get it. But what do you think happened to me that night?"

"Well, I think that the power you started to feel brought up a lot of fear – fear from that lifetime in Atlantis. The crystal skulls did want you to have an understanding of the dark. You need that understanding to be aware of these things and how to protect yourself. It's important to recognize what's really going on. This is the knowledge and wisdom that will enable you to work with power and become powerful."

She paused to sip her tea and then continued.

"The other thing is about you wanting to push yourself to have an experience – to not be satisfied with how much you have already received. The thing is that there's nothing that's holding you back in the first place – except your own understanding and lack of self-worth. You had a powerful experience with the skull working on you – you said it felt like acupuncture and you ended up learning so much of how energy operates not only on the body but on this planet as well. That's an amazing revelation; yet, you haven't even allowed for that whole process to integrate. When you make a bid for knowledge and power, the skulls will come to you - but so much of what this work is about is right timing, as you've already come to realize. And one more thing, Eliot: in all our striving for greater knowledge, power and service to humanity, we must not lose sight of our humility and gratitude for all that we have already received."

I felt very humbled after that, yet also very well. I sat upright on the sofa and understood about not beating yourself up.

"When you were sitting in the center of the circle, how many skulls did you see around you?" Mia asked.

"Twelve, I said.

"And what about the thirteenth skull?"

I paused. "I know now that the thirteenth skull is our own human skull – it represents humanity. We sit at the center and it is our consciousness, our own crystalline skull that must awaken for the Golden Age to be made manifest."

"And so it is," she replied.

CHAPTER TEN

The next day I awoke with my head full and, as usual, I needed to process. The difficult experience of facing the dark was behind me now but, as with all experiences of an esoteric nature, it opens up other doorways in your psyche. It amazes me how we underestimate the ability of our unconscious to sabotage ourselves. Yet having said that, I realize that it is those very errors in judgment that lead us to a greater sense of awareness. They enable us to delve more deeply, not only into ourselves, but into the whole of the human condition.

It felt good to be back in Penzance. Penzance, Cornwall - I liked the sound of that and still do. By the time I can see St. Michael's Mount in the distance, as I drive into Penzance, a sense of peace envelopes me. That landmark seems to stand there as a guide to the land you are about to enter. Located at the southernmost tip of England, the smell of the sea and the song of seagulls seem to carry messages from that mount down to the villagers and back up again. I likened it to Mount Olympus, but in a much smaller version. Instead of Zeus and Hera up there at the helm, I pictured Margaret and Mia.

"You know, Mia, I've been thinking a lot about drugs and what people are searching for when they take them."

"In what way? I don't really know much about recreational drugs."

I felt my mind wander again. For how long I cannot say.

"Eliot, are you listening?"

I couldn't help but smile at the images of Mount Olympus I had conjured up. Regaining my composure, I brought myself back down to reality.

"Sorry, I guess I was somewhere else. Where were we?"

"You were starting to say something about recreational drugs before you stopped speaking altogether."

"Right. Well, I was referring to mind altering drugs like Ecstasy or E, as they call it now. Anyway, E opens your heart but that feeling is short lived and artificial. It drains you and leaves you feeling quite depleted and depressed afterwards. I can understand why people want to take drugs for the very reason that they want to expand their consciousness – that's what I was trying to do the couple of times I tried it. As an anthropologist, I figured that I should experiment, so Stephen and I did. But I always knew that it wasn't something to mess around with. There are cultures, of course, that use certain herbs to induce particular states of consciousness. I was thinking about regular folk and what would happen if they would only delve into these things naturally. Well, we'd be living in quite a different world!"

"Yes, because somewhere in our collective memory, we remember that we once lived in a time where we could experience these different states of consciousness easily. Unfortunately, most people are seeking only an outward connection whether it's drugs or alcohol or some other form of escapism, rather than turning inwardly. I've never thought of escaping outside of myself. Instead, I needed the opposite, to remain focused on staying in my body."

"Yes, I can see that it would be the reverse for you," I said, smiling at her.

"I hadn't thought of it in that way before but I guess you have a point. What was that saying Timothy Leary made famous in the Sixties?"

"You mean, "tune in, turn on and drop out," I said.

"Yes, that's it. But something doesn't quite fit – the turning on and dropping out part. I think it was misguided," Mia said, as she dipped her toast in her egg.

We were sitting in her kitchen having breakfast. English style, of course, with baked beans, fried tomatoes, eggs, sausages for me, and heaps of toast with Marmite and marmalade.

"I can understand the 'dropping out' part, at least for the Summer of Love generation. It's the sense of wanting something altogether different from your parent's generation. You know, that stoic, straight-laced conservative attitude and the fact that it was a movement of expression, of being completely different from what came before."

"Yes, I can see that as well," she said. "That's all well and good but how can you hold on to an experience when there isn't a base to stand on? You can't just take a substance and think that's going to enlighten you. Unless, like you said, you come from a culture where you are under the guidance and tutelage of a shaman or a person like that."

"Margaret once explained to me," I replied, "that if you don't work on yourself, the energy goes in but won't stay because you haven't made room for it to stay. I think the same applies to drugs. Most spiritual experiences don't happen through the intellect but rather the knowledge is revealed through all of your senses. It isn't localized in any particular area, at least it wasn't for me."

"Yes" she responded quietly. "And it is those exquisite, brief glimpses of the universe in its entirety that keep us searching only to rediscover it again and again. This knowledge, or insight, is so powerful, its meaning can only be grasped in that precise moment. We retain the multisensory memory of what it means to truly 'know' in the form of that experience. However, the knowledge of how to return to that place, to sustain the experience, may once again be hidden from us."

"Except for those who are already enlightened," I said.

"Well, yes. Thankfully, we have some powerful teachers out there. I'm so grateful that I can also work with the skulls using them as a tool to help me retain some of this knowledge."

Mia seemed to be stating the obvious but I didn't say anything, just giving a nod in agreement. I knew she wanted to convey more so I sat there eating, listening to the sound of her voice, observing the way her eyes would widen when she was animated.

"There are three different types of spiritual initiations that you can experience when working with the skulls. They are known as the rays of love, light and power," Mia continued.

"Rays?" I asked.

"Yes, think of the word 'emanation' or 'energy' as another way of describing it. You have experienced all three. Each of these rays contains infinite knowledge. In terms of accessing their knowledge, it depends on who you are and what ray or energy you resonate with the most."

I paused for a moment, thinking about what she had said. I knew that I had experienced all three types of initiation but I wanted to sort them out in my head before responding.

Mia waited for me to continue, much like the way a teacher would do if you'd only half answered a question. It is the teacher's way of gauging whether or not you've understood the subject matter. She waited patiently for me to reply.

I did take my time, reminding myself that this was not a test. I found that I could relax so much more with Mia now. When you've allowed someone to see you at your most vulnerable and they're still there at the end of it, you know that a barrier has forever been dismantled.

"I experienced the ray of power when I was shown the darkness. But I would also have to say just experiencing the black skull would be an initiation into the ray of power."

"Exactly. When you think of the energy of black and all that it contains, just to have the black skull come through to commune with you is powerful. The black skull does not work with just anyone, you know. It has to call you to it and, in a sense, you have to want to be called."

"It's fascinating really because I can also see how the black skull has so much love and light within it," I said.

"Yes, it's just that the doorway into the skull is through the vibration of power. That doesn't mean to say that you are not open to love or the intellect. As the skulls repeatedly explain, you have to be in balance and the black skull has an affinity working with power and power issues."

"I am assuming when you say the rays of light, you are talking about knowledge and wisdom and the intellect," I said.

"Yes, that's right."

I closed my eyes and took it all in.

I spoke carefully, "then what you are saying, really, is that the skulls interface. They are all connected to each other. It makes sense that when you work with the skulls that you would sit in the center of a circle – because a circle implies that there is no beginning, middle or end. And as you sit there, you can feel just how their energies merge and form new patterns. And it is those new patterns which enable us to see into something – some knowledge or aspect that may not have been tapped into before. I would imagine that that is what a scientific discovery would look like if we had the ability to watch the expression of the thought form in action."

"What an interesting analogy, Eliot. What you've just described would be a perfect example of what it's like to work with the ray of light. It doesn't mean that it's the intellect that is of importance. On the contrary, it's that you are open to understanding concepts with your intellect that then translate into manifestation. The ray of light has to do with inspiration from all sources. And the light skull would, of course, be the skull to work with in developing those qualities."

"And what about the ray of love? What skull would you attribute that to?"

"I would attribute that to the rose quartz crystal skull," she said. "I know we haven't really talked about that skull yet, nor the others and how they all interface, and that's only because there is so much to tap into with just the light and the black. For now, that is what is most important, not just for your personal development, but for what is needed on the planet at this time. We live in such a place of duality, people not having the understanding of the light and dark in all of their aspects." Mia was still for a moment and then continued.

"Having said that, the rose quartz crystal skull *is* as important as the light and black skull because it's love that transforms us and, quite simply, makes us better human beings. Think of the rose quartz skull as the connection in the center between the black and the light skull. The energy is so soft. I know that you have experienced it because you told me how you felt such peace that evening that we called all the crystal skulls. The rose skull is so gentle. Think of what rose quartz looks like, the softness of it. It is non-invasive. Now imagine a crystal skull made of rose quartz.

It may be present, and you may not recognize it at first because it catches you unawares. It is incredibly powerful but a power that is so refined - the kind of power that stops you in your tracks because of its beauty." Mia paused here and I could see she felt deeply about what she had said. She took a deep breath and let it out slowly.

"A beauty, Eliot, which takes your breath away. Beauty, real beauty, can melt even the hardest of hearts. When you are graced with that much love, in all her forms, and emanate that, you truly are a force to be reckoned with. So when you want healing, or knowledge that has to do with all things of the heart, call in the rose quartz crystal skull. She will guide you. So imagine the light skull above you, the black skull beneath you, and the rose quartz skull right in the center. That is a powerful meditation in and of itself — you are in perfect balance then."

While Mia had been speaking about the rose skull, something started to happen to me. My heart had naturally opened. That is how the rose quartz skull reaches you. I could feel my heart receiving her. I sat there listening to Mia, all the while feeling more and more open.

"I met this man," Mia continued. "He was the kind of man that I thought was right for me. In fact, he looked and seemed a lot like you - tall, fair hair, blue eyes, even wore similar glasses. He was intelligent, fun to be around. He had a way with words and I loved listening to him. But he was nothing like you. He had a quality that attracted me to him but I can see now that I was really searching for you but hadn't realized it. Although I did learn a lot from that relationship."

Mia looked at me then to see if I understood. I thought of how I had chosen to be with similar types of women, like Heather and Tina, as Stephen had pointed out to me. Being with those two women had enabled me to work on particular aspects of myself that I could not have done on my own. Some human qualities can only be drawn out in relationship while others develop best in solitude. And when you're done learning those lessons you can finally attract your soul mate who will guide you in the next phase of your development.

"I guess I got lost in the projection of what I wanted our relationship to be," Mia said. It was a hard lesson to realize how much of myself I had put aside in order to be someone I wasn't. I was pretty heartbroken and feeling such a fool for being drawn into a fantasy. It's not very often that I find someone that I think I can relate to."

She had been relaying all this with her eyes off in the distance but now looked straight at me.

"One evening, I sat in the center of the circle calling all of the ancient crystal skulls to come and be with me. I had called them in for guidance and it wasn't easy. My request seemed trivial in the grand scheme of things but when your heart is broken, it is raw and painful as we all know too well. You can't deny it yet you don't know how to move forward. It doesn't seem to matter what you're blessed with, what you already know, what you're in the process of learning. There are times when there is no consolation. And those unwanted feelings, too numerous and unbearable to face, keep taking you off center. It was a never-ending cycle, it seemed, and I couldn't be still and switch them off.

So there I was feeling fragile and unnerved. I went into the circle in the guise of a priestess thinking surely I should be beyond caring if a mere male mortal did not return the love I offered."

I smiled inwardly at her choice of words. They were dramatic and the tone of her voice implied she was making fun of herself – of how we not only get caught up in the heartbreak but also how our egos suffer quite a beating in the process.

"Nevertheless," Mia continued, "my reality, in that instance, was quite different from what I thought it ought to have been. It's one thing to help others through feelings of inadequacy and loss with compassion and without judgment and quite another when my own wounds are burning and won't heal. It was difficult then for me to be still enough to reach the place of the skulls but I sat there waiting all the same."

Mia rose and picked up her cup of tea walking into the living room and sat cross-legged once again on her favorite armchair. I followed right behind and took my place on the sofa. It was late morning and, although cold, the sun shone filling the room with light and warmth.

I could tell that here, now, was the priestess recounting her story. It wasn't just Mia any longer. I do not even know if she noticed but I was there with her feeling her sadness and all of the love bestowed upon her, past and present, in equal measure. I could sense it from both the place in which I sat and from the perspective of being there in the circle, watching the scene as it unfolded.

Her heart is visible for all to see. It beats to the rhythm of a bird that has fallen out of its nest, harboring a broken wing. She cannot see how beautiful she looks or how big her heart is at this moment – so big, it looks out of proportion to the rest of her. And as she sits there in the center of the circle, the rose quartz crystal skull moves towards her. It is so gentle that she does not realize that the skull has approached her. Her heart, however, recognizes this presence and welcomes it. It enters softly and catches her unawares; she breathes a sigh of release and a sigh of comfort and she begins to tune into the very soft but deeply penetrating energy of the rose quartz crystal skull.

All she can hear is the sound of her heart beating. The sound is so loud it drowns out the voices of despair in her head and those feelings lose their way. The sound is no different than that of a beating drum. She is so enthralled that, as she follows its rhythm, it carries her back to the beginning when she was not yet born but very much alive. She finds herself suspended in warmth gestating in a place that feels like a mother's womb. It is not as dark a place as one might expect. There is a soft pink light, ever-present and glowing.

She is so open now. Her mind is clear. She is still. The particulars of her everyday life no longer matter. She understands that what is important is this feeling, this peace that resides within her now. And then she remembers why she has come, the sharpness of her pierced heart brings her back to the question, the answer to which she longs to know. She lowers her head in shame. How can she ask the skull?

The rose quartz crystal skull is resting there in front of her, glowing so much that a soft pink light forms a protective shield around her. It is as if a warm blanket has just been placed around her shoulders. She both hears the response in her head and feels it in her heart.

Do not be ashamed. The words flow into her like a song carrying such tenderness that the tears begin to fall down her face. *Can you not see how big your heart is? It is meant for loving. You feel the pain of rejection because your heart is so open and the rest of you has not yet caught up to the bigness of your heart. It is not the other way round. It is your mind, your desires and your ego that feeds the pain. The moment you first felt love for this person, you loved completely and totally for you glimpsed the soul. And in that glimpse, you recognized yourself mirrored in the other. That is why in loving someone, you love yourself and in loving yourself, you love others. It is the moments that come after that first meeting with someone else's heart that take us off-center and make us confused. Sometimes, the other person glimpses your heart, too, and a romantic dance begins. The dance may last for only a moment or it may last many years. It does not matter. It is the act of loving, in whatever form it takes that matters. The moment was presented so that you could feel and see love mirrored back to you in the shape of this person. If the love that you offer is not reciprocated, mourn the loss and see that it was meant for the moment in which it was felt. Allow for the love you have given to be transformed. It will come back and find you, renewed, offering itself to you in a different form. So be open and proud of your loving.*

She does not feel so ashamed now. It was her loss of pride that flushed her cheeks and made her feel foolish. Sometimes, the healing comes simply by someone else acknowledging that pain.

The rose quartz skull has receded back into the circle with all the other crystal skulls. They form a protective shield around her. She sits and waits to be transported into another time and place. I was honored that she shared something so intimate with me and that intimacy is what brought me to the ray of love once again.

This time though, there was a different quality to it. It is not very often we have the opportunity to be a witness inside someone's heart – a memory I shall keep dear in my own. Somehow, we made our way back into the kitchen. Mia grabbed the stool that she used to reach those high places. She stood on it and I held her close for as long as I could. I would soon be leaving for London.

CHAPTER ELEVEN

This time when I took the skull out of the museum, put it in its carrying case and placed it on the floor of the passenger side of my car, I knew that I was doing the right thing. This time it wasn't about me – what I thought, what I wanted. This time I was doing it for her. I knew that I had to take the skull to Mia and that this was the opportunity I had been waiting for. I realized the time that I took the skull home with me was really a precursor for this – that it had given me the courage and strength I needed to travel a much further distance with it. I got that I was meant to take it all the way down to Cornwall to see the one person who truly knew how to connect with it. This had been my destiny all along.

It had only been a couple of weeks since the last time I had seen Mia. She was going to be travelling soon and I wanted to spend as much time as possible with her before that occurred. So I left well before dawn and headed for Lamorna, to Margaret's place. Margaret was away and Mia was staying there for a few days looking after Ajax.

"I have a surprise for you; will you do me the honor?" I said to her when I arrived at her doorstep. She was dressed in a deep olive green, a color which suited her and often wore. A measuring tape was draped around her neck like a fashionable accessory. She had been sewing and I could hear soft music in the background.

"Why, yes," she said, taken aback.

"Then let me go on up to the sitting room," I said, gently pushing my way past her. "I'll call you when it's time to come up."

She shook her head in bewilderment and closed the front door. She did as I bid her. I picked up the case along with a bag I had brought with me, finished my preparations and called for her to come upstairs.

She fell silent when she stepped into the room.

I had placed the skull on top of the coffee table with 12 tea lights surrounding it, the burning incense enhancing the atmosphere of the altar I had put together.

And then she spoke calmly, enunciating every word.

"Eliot, I don't think you've heard anything I've ever said to you. I'm going to take Ajax out for a walk now because I'm not quite sure what I'm going to say to you when I return. But whatever it is, you'd better be ready to listen."

I was dumfounded! This wasn't what I had expected. I looked at the skull which seemed to be grinning. My heart sank and I followed her as she climbed down the stairs with Ajax at her heels. He too seemed upset with me.

"Please, don't follow me." And with that she took her coat and stormed out.

I needed a cigarette. I went down to the garden and smoked, inhaling deeply as I paced up and down the length of the garden. There was nothing soothing in the sound of the brook today. I couldn't understand why Mia was so upset. I thought that I had given her the gift that rightfully belonged to her. I was confused and disheartened.

I made a fire and blew out the candles while waiting for Mia to return. Had I unwittingly transgressed the boundary of some ancient sacred rite? How had I offended her? None of it made any sense to me. Mia returned a good hour later. Her cheeks were flushed from the cold. I was glad that I had made a fire as I knew that warmth was needed in more ways than one.

I stood up when she entered.

"Would you sit down, Eliot?" she said crisply.

She stood by the fire warming herself and I sat opposite feeling like a schoolboy about to be scolded.

"I didn't mean to be disrespectful." I said. "If I have done something to offend you. I am truly sorry."

"Oh, Eliot, this isn't about me. I can see that you wished to please me. But can't you see that you've taken matters into your own hands again?" She said pleadingly.

I was about to speak but she held up her hand. The words froze in my throat.

"You don't have the right to take the skull out of the museum. You could go to prison for this. And what if you'd had an accident? I could go on and on. I thought that I had. That you had learned your lesson."

"Mia, you are right. But please, let me speak," I said, my confidence returning.

"Take a look at the skull, Mia. It's glowing." And indeed it was. The candles were not lit, the sun was not reflecting off of it. In fact, it was overcast outside. But the skull was beaming and the light grew bigger.

"I thought of all the years you had spent going to visit the skull at the museum and not being able to touch it or meditate with it in private. This I can give to you. This past year you have given me so much. You have given me a purpose, given me back my life, Mia."

She opened her mouth to speak but this time I held up my hand. I wanted her to listen.

"There are no words that I can find to thank you for everything you've done for me – the support, the love and the encouragement. You trusted in me when I didn't trust in myself and believed in me when I didn't even know there was something to believe in. You have made me see that greatness is something of which we are all capable and that we don't need to stay lost forever. This is my way of showing you my gratitude."

I didn't give her time to speak, I had more to say.

"Even more importantly, I heard a voice in my head. All it said was: *It is time*. In that instant, I knew what that meant. I could see this room, the table laid out exactly as it is now. It was all right to take the skull out of the museum. I knew no one would understand or allow this to happen but I also understood what you meant about spiritual laws. Because, Mia, it was the skull who directed me to do this and I knew there would be no repercussions. I knew, and know still, the skull would be protected. You and I needed to be here, not in London where I could have given you a private viewing at the museum, without any repercussions.

I knew we needed to be here, in this place by the brook and the woods surrounding us. This place is powerful. Margaret called it a vortex. The timing is right and the time is now. And you, Mia, know that better than anyone."

She softened then and understood. She approached the skull and gently touched it, taking it all in with her hands.

For the first time, I understood what it felt like to be speaking not as the Eliot that I know so well but as Eliot, the priest, the one who assists the divine feminine in balance and unity.

I spoke softly and continued.

"I have known for a while that we would perform a sacred rite. It was Margaret who first mentioned it when we were in this very room, when I became acquainted with the black skull but I purposely didn't ask any questions. I kept them somewhere in the back of my mind and knew that the day would come when you would enlighten me. To be honest, it sounded a bit intimidating in the sense that I couldn't see myself in that role. All I could do was be present in the moment. But my heart did leap in excitement. I don't know how I've managed to push that aside for all these months but I did. I just knew not to go there. So here I am, Mia. I'm ready now."

"Yes, I can see that. You've created the sacred space for us. And when the work is done, the skull will be returned to the museum?"

"All right," I said and paused for a while, then continued, "I think I've always understood the importance of sacred space, of honoring that which you hold dear to your heart. When I was a boy, my parents took me to India. My father was on a business trip. All I remember was being inside of this Buddhist temple in Delhi. We walked in and I saw this colossal Buddha. I was very small - who knows how big it really was - but to me, it was huge.

I stood there, looking up at his face. His eyes were closed and there was an exquisite and serene smile on his face. I think that he was smiling to the Divine from the inside. I did not know who this man was but I could tell that he must have been a man of greatness to have a statue made in his likeness, with offerings of devotion laid out at his feet.

It was a strange and wondrous place. My eyes and mouth were wide open as I took it all in. There were so many incense sticks burning that the smell was making me dizzy but I liked it nevertheless.

I wondered at the many bowls of rice, cooked and uncooked - so beautifully arranged around the altar. There were also flowers and delicacies with which I was not familiar. The vibrancy of the colors and the love in which the offerings were displayed made it the most enchanting place I had ever visited. But I wondered how it was that food would be offered so freely to a statue when there were those living that needed it more. It was a concept that I was able to barely grasp but I questioned this nonetheless. I made the connection because of the people so desperate for food, the beggars I had seen outside. Even the cows, as beautiful as they were, treated with the utmost respect, looked as if they too could have done with more food.

"I have held on to the memory of this temple ever since and it is the reason I became an anthropologist. I always knew it was the Buddha's smile that had something to do with the answer I have been seeking. However, it wasn't until this moment that I understood the answer."

Mia looked up at me. She seemed to be glowing, just as the skull was, and I knew it wasn't just because of the skull's presence but because we were sharing our deepest joys and revelations.

"Creating an altar is an expression of divinity, a way of showing that we place our faith in them. By offering something of the material to spirit, by giving the things that nourish and please us most, we can express our gratitude and faith that what we need will be given unto us. When you light a candle, whether it's in a church or a cathedral, in a spiritual ceremony or on your own personal altar, it is the intention with which you light that candle that sends your prayer up and carries your devotion to be received and blessed.

For years, I sought to find the source of the Buddha's smile. I tried intellectually but now, as I approach mid-life, I realize that I have found that smile in the oddest of places - from that temple in Delhi to this self-made one. Creating this space for you is my expression of what the skulls and you, as their priestess, have shown me. What you seek is always inside of you. The deepest of mysteries can be revealed when you look inside and find the Divine within. That door into your heart is right there waiting until such time that you choose to open it."

Mia listened and I could hear the stream below and I imagined that it too was listening, carrying my thoughts and feelings to the sea. And after what seemed like the silence of an age, I continued, "Tell me about the black and white checkered tiles."

"The black and white tiles belong to a place known as the Akasha. The tiles are the floor upon which the Akasha stands, its foundation so to speak."

I looked at her, puzzled. Her eyes shifted from the skull and she gazed slightly to her right, as if the explanation would come to her from that direction. I gave her time to compose her thoughts.

"The Akasha doesn't actually exist anywhere in the world, yet it exists everywhere. It is a place that is built upon the essence of all that is. The skulls can be likened to a tangible expression of the Akasha in the sense that within each skull dwells the information of humanity. The Akasha then holds the information of all that ever was, is and will be - not only of our universe but of the cosmos. The Akasha is also referred to as the Hall of Wisdom, the Hall of Records or the Akashic Records. Imagine it to be like the greatest library in the universe. Anything and everything you've ever wanted to know is there. But you can't just get there by simply wanting to go there and finding out the secrets of the universe. The secrets are revealed to those initiated into these mysteries, but only to the level of their spiritual comprehension. You cannot go beyond where you haven't yet reached."

She paused to give me time to think but I could see that she had a lot more to say. When discussing esoteric teachings something extraordinary begins to happen. You have heard this before, glimpsing these hidden truths somewhere in the periphery of your mind. Excitement builds and the atmosphere around you changes. It's as if you are being held in a protective bubble where your energy expands to soak up this information. The energy is malleable - it moves and breathes as you move and breathe. Becoming aware of this opens you up further so that you feel safe and pure in the reception of the knowledge.

"The Akasha is not only a library in that sense, but also a place where magic happens. It is a place where you can open yourself up to receive the knowledge of the universe, ingest and digest what you wish to convey and then make manifest from the spiritual realms to the material plane. Ritual, then, is the expression of this.

"Ritual is something we do every day of our lives. We get up at a certain time; we go to work at another time; we have our tea or coffee at yet another time. Ritual is what gives structure to our day and makes us feel secure in the routines of our lives. And there is another kind of ritual, sacred ritual. It's the kind of ritual you experience at a mass, baptism, wedding, or an official ceremony of some kind. These sacred rituals are what connects us to Spirit, giving our lives meaning and focus. They are a way of healing imbalances and addressing sanctity. So when you stand upon the floor of the Hall of Wisdom, know that you are in a sacred place and in a temple of manifestation."

I paused for a moment, to take it all in.

"And what was that great big book that I had read from?" I asked her.

"Remember there are many doorways or gateways into the Hall of Wisdom. The skulls are one portal into this dimension. When you met me, you had a memory of me and that memory was the beginning of your remembrance of the skulls. A connection was made and that evening, you were open to receive. The great book is another way by which you can see into the Akasha. Some do not need to look at the book but can simply stand in the Hall and what they need to know will be revealed to them. Think of the book as a symbol where the knowledge is contained. Every person on this planet can read from this book but only what is pertinent to each one's spiritual growth. There is an energy or force contained within the pages of the book. Your spirit must be in alignment with this, the only way in which you will be able to access the knowledge. It is the same with the skulls."

I sat there listening, remembering that time and realized that in the Dreamtime, we go to the Hall of Wisdom. When you experience déjà vu, receiving an impression, or a feeling of what is to come, it is because you have already seen it in the Akasha. The same is true when you meet someone and they seem so familiar, although you have never met them before. I understood that the Akasha was a place of great learning and when we are in our deepest sleep, or quiet in meditation, we go to this place for insight and healing.

Mia went on, "There is a shift happening on our planet. We are coming up to a very special time in our history. We have the capacity to change fate, to realign once again to that time long ago when there was peace and unity. But it will be different and will reflect what we have become now in this time and place. Great change is upon us - on many, many levels. We have been out of balance for far too long. The black skull and the light skull, as well as the other crystal skulls, have been waiting for this moment to assist energetically in realigning us to unity. We were once androgynous beings - carrying both the male and female aspects within us. We carry that still - our animus, if we are women, or our anima, if we are men, as Jung taught. The side hidden from us can make us feel lost so we search for that unity outside of ourselves in the form of a mate or, sometimes, through other external diversions. So much discontent and unhappiness stem from that separation of self. But that other half is inside of us. We seek a mate and many times become disappointed because, after a while, they no longer reflect what we thought they were to us. It is our own inner anima or animus that we seek to connect with. And so the dance of the polarities begins. The male and the female, not quite knowing how to find each other even when they are looking into each other's eyes, search in all the wrong places.

When you can find the balance within yourself, you can draw the right person to you because your spirits will be in harmony, your inner and outer expression of the masculine and the feminine will complement and enhance one another's. And some may wish to live truly as themselves not needing the reflection from another but rather carrying both aspects within and without."

Mia moved and stretched, and then walked towards the window. "Let us call in the light skull and the black skull now to assist us in achieving this balance. When we go to the Hall of Wisdom, we will be there not only as Mia and Eliot, but as all women and all men, healing not only our own imbalances, but those of the collective as well – the receptive and dynamic forces invoked in harmony. That is the role of the priestess and her priest."

❧

THE HALL OF WISDOM

There appears to be nothing in the room until you step inside and start to walk. It is as if you are blindfolded - not knowing what direction to take or what lies waiting. Your heart beats rapidly with apprehension and excitement. The clothes you once wore are left behind - on the outside of the room - where your life, as you know it, awaits your return.

Mia is dressed entirely in black and I, Eliot, in white.

The particulars of the clothes do not matter. What is of importance are the colors - black and white. Look down at your feet and see that your shoes also match the color of your garment. Then, notice the floor upon which you stand – a black and white checkered floor, stretching to infinity.

Stand there for a moment and become familiar with this place. Let your senses be your guide, opening you up to seeing with your hands and feet and throat and ears and nose. Feel the tingling at the base of your skull. Feel your third eye open from inside like flicking open the shutters of a lens. Feel your solar plexus expanding, supporting you in place.

Begin to notice how easy it is to follow the rhythm of your breath. This is a quiet place, a place of healing, a place of knowledge and a place of no time. The light skull and the black skull are in front of you. You can almost see them pulsating with power as they settle there, awaiting the work at hand.

As you focus your attention on the black skull, you begin to feel activity behind you, like a warm breeze blowing. You do not have to turn around as you can see everything from the base of your skull. Your ancestors – all those that have gone before and all those that are supporting you in your growth have come, at this moment, to assist you and welcome your magnificence into the Hall of Wisdom.

Let your ancestors be your support and guide. They understand you and you, them, for you are the physical embodiment of all that they are. It is a special lineage - a precious lineage and a great lineage because it is yours. Feel from how far back they have come to be here with you. Some have come for healing and forgiveness. Others have come as observers but most have come to assist you in your growth. For as you develop and grow, so, too, do they develop and grow.

All that you are and all that you will be is held within the very fabric of the walls and floor and ceiling of this room. As you step forward onto a new black or white marble tile, a growth in your con-sciousness occurs. Your mind and your body open to receive this new awareness of ancient memories surfacing from the base of your skull.

The ancestors form two lines, one to your right and one to your left. The formation they make is that of two very large wings. And as *they take their places, they transform and become your wings. See the intricacy of the pattern of the wings. Feel how many feathers make up each wing. Although there are so many, they are light and it is their strength that carries you forward. Get used to your new wings. Move them about and feel how their tips brush lightly against your cheek and your hair, as if you are gently being kissed. It is the kiss of tenderness that you have waited an eternity to remember and to feel.*

In this place you are free — outside of duality and outside of time. The lightness of your wings can carry you to wherever you wish to go. So fly and be free. Spread your wings as far back as they will go so that you may see yourself and be truly admired — like a peacock, but the patterns and shapes you carry are so much more intricate and refined. Open and close your wings so that it cleanses your soul — back and forth rhythmically swaying so that you cleanse and renew the spirit of your lineage. The flapping of your wings creates new rhythms and new patterns of light - fanning out the darkness and welcoming in the light. Renewed of spirit, your wings carry you forward, down onto a new black or white tile, in the great Hall of Wisdom.

Notice the light beings standing in front of you to your right, behind the light skull. They form the shape of an inverted pyramid. These are your future selves. The light that they carry is so bright that it may be difficult to see what is in front of you. Just breathe in deeply and be patient. They have come to assist you in awakening so that you may understand and know.

Make yourself known to them so that they recognize you and that you may get to know them. You are so open and light that you can receive them in such a way that you have never before experienced. Feel the tingling from the base of your skull moving up and down your spine - this sensation is your DNA awakening. Allow for your future selves to guide you, to show you what is of importance in your evolution, because they have already been where you now stand.

Stand in the middle of the light skull and the black skull - evolution and regeneration meeting, in just the right measure - in the space beyond time. Focus on where you wish to go, what you wish to see, to heal, to understand - from the past to the present to the future. And, as you stand there in the middle of the light skull and the black skull, feel the power of your past behind you and the power of your future in front of you. Their combined force melds into you and moves you with lightning speed to where you need to go.

With all that you are, you can create and affect change in your mind, your body and your spirit. When you are renewed, see how you have shifted onto another tile in the great Hall of Wisdom.

All is as it should be. This place exists, remember it and know.

⚘

Time does not exist in this place; yet we were there for what seemed an eternity. Moving, dancing, making love, upon the marble floor that had become the foundation upon which the enactment of the sacred marriage was staged.

CHAPTER TWELVE

"There is a Native American legend which says that when all thirteen ancient crystal skulls are found, we will enter into a Golden Age of peace and wisdom," I said to Mia. "I heard about this from a group of people who had come to view the skull in the museum. This was a while back and, at the time, I didn't really pay that much attention to it because I didn't understand what they meant. But then when I had my own experience sitting in the center of the circle and you had asked me how many skulls I had seen, I clearly saw twelve and I knew that I represented the thirteenth. I hadn't thought about that until this moment. What do you think about this legend?"

"I think what is of importance here is the skull in the center – *yours* – and that you need to be in harmony for the wisdom to be revealed to you. It doesn't matter whether they have all been found; what is of importance is that humanity awakens to the knowledge. We have been given an extraordinary gift – great insights occurring not only in our minds but in our hearts as well. The Golden Age won't happen in the blink of an eye but we can choose to move in that direction. Many people have chosen this path already and many more will follow."

"Imagine, then," Mia continued "that we are sitting in the center of a circle with all the ancient crystal skulls around us. The skulls have, of course, already been found because we know of this place where we can access them energetically. Align yourself to what the Golden Age means, what an age of peace might actually feel like. This is how you journey into the future."

The atmosphere had changed and this feeling, by now familiar, no longer brought questions or doubt but an openness to receive what was being offered. This was the morning after our most sacred time together.

I felt peaceful. Peacefulness, I once thought, was a state where not much happens but you are simply present to enjoy the moment, like sitting in meditation. I realized as I sat there in the center of that circle with Mia beside me and all the ancient crystal skulls surrounding us, that this wasn't true at all. Peacefulness can bring quietude and contemplation but it doesn't mean that you do nothing. In fact, a lot was happening to me and what I observed was that I was in a place of unity and within that unity, all was possible.

I had my eyes closed for a long time and when I opened them again, I found that the twelve skulls had transformed into the twelve constellations of our galaxy. They were represented by the symbols we are familiar with. I noticed that I sat directly opposite the water bearer, the symbol for Aquarius. She was a woman with a vessel that was filled to the brim with water and, as the water flowed out from the jar, a pool formed around her so that she looked as if she were part of the most exquisite fountain. Leo, the lion, was behind me. His eyes sparkled like emerald jewels and the soft breeze that blew enabled me to see how thick and luxurious his golden mane was.

To my left was a great bull, known as Taurus. He had steam coming out of his nostrils and he wore a thick gold ring in it for adornment. He smelled of the earth, of the freshness of tilled soil. To my right was the eagle, representing the sign of Scorpio. At first, the eagle was a scorpion. It changed a few times from scorpion to eagle and back again until it shifted for the last time and settled in place as the eagle, the highest manifestation of this deeply mysterious sign. These four fixed symbols formed a cross of energy and there we sat inside of a circle, in the center of a cross. Had you been looking down upon us from above, you would have seen a cross of light with Mia and I in the center, sitting in unity as a single rose.

"Focus on the water bearer," I heard Mia's voice sounding as if she herself was immersed in water. I did as she bid me and the water bearer shifted and transformed into the light crystal skull. The skull was both in front of me and placed on top of my own skull. It felt as if I had placed a crown on top of my head that had molded itself to my own face.

The beauty about this work and this knowledge is that there are so many ways to go about it. All have meaning and purpose. As I sat there in the center of the circle, I could feel how the light of the skull was creating prisms within my very own soul, illuminating that which I had kept hidden for a long time.

I thought of the passage in the Bible: 'In my Father's house are many mansions.' All the great religions, all the spiritual teachings have been brought to humanity as gifts. Since there are so many different cultures, there are many expressions to the divine force that reins us all. For thousands of years, we have forgotten this truth, each believing that our way was the only way. This is how the dogma of righteousness and separation began to tear us apart.

I could see that in the Golden Age, the truth of each religion and spiritual teaching will be honored. Depending upon the spiritual maturity of the individual, he or she will work towards their own personal evolution as well as that of the greater collective.

I could see that the crystal skulls had travelled back in time from this age of peace and wisdom, waiting for the moment when we could understand their teachings.

I had a vision then of the great teachers of the Golden Age gathered in a circle, the skulls placed in a smaller circle inside their own. They were using their love, light and power to shape and form their thoughts into the crystalline structures before them. The sound of the most exquisite symphony was heard as this transfer of knowledge and energy took place and the light that poured forth was brilliant to behold.

Then I heard a voice. I knew that it was actually a chorus but with such perfect harmony that it sounded like one voice:

To all those incarnated at this time, you have all been given a mission and that is to assist in the spiritual evolution of your beloved planet and her inhabitants. This is a special mission and one that you have chosen to embark upon whether you are consciously aware of it or not. It is time now to remember and to be in service to your true Self for that is the way to be of service to others, having all that you need to give and receive in joy and abundance. It does not matter who you are or where you have come from. All you need is an open heart. Dream yourself awake.

∿

I had become a witness then, to the past and the future and now, very much anchored in the present. I am not the man I was before the veil parted some 18 months ago. Margaret once said to me that others wouldn't recognize me as the change would be so great. But I recognize myself more now than all those years before the skulls and Mia had come into my life. Mia has accepted an invitation to New Zealand. She was in contact with another guardian so her work continues in many different ways.

I stayed in Lamorna for a few more days with Mia and I enjoying each other's company in the simplicity of life as it presented itself to us. We drove up together to London and parted at Heathrow, embracing for as long as time permitted.

"Till we meet again," she said.

I gazed at her and all that needed to be said between us was reflected back to me in the warmth of her smile.

The skull has a new home in the museum. I found the perfect spot, although there isn't natural sunlight and it has to be encased - but I do my best. I have taken it upon my-self to catalogue artifacts that have their own mystery to convey. And the ones that I can place near the skull, I do. I watch the interaction and take notes of how this can be of relevance later on, when museums will be ready for this type of work.

Margaret and I have forged a deep friendship and visit one another as often as we can. Even Stephen has jour-neyed down to Lamorna to visit with Margaret and the de-lightful Ajax. I don't know when Mia will return, I half expect her to walk into the museum as she used to do. She will come and visit us both this time. Of that, I am sure.

EPILOGUE

There is a crystal skull in the British Museum known as the British Museum crystal skull. The description in this novel is, in fact, of the famed Mitchell-Hedges crystal skull, with which I have used poetic license.

I first met Anna Mitchell-Hedges in 1995 when she lived in Kitchener, Ontario, Canada. Many may know her story of how she discovered the crystal skull. But for those of you who do not, below is what she recounted to me on several occasions. Some do not believe Anna's story. There is evidence to suggest that the skull was auctioned at Sotheby's and that her adoptive father, F.A. Mitchell-Hedges, bought it several years after their expedition.

Anna explained to me that one of her father's pastimes was buying and selling antiques, especially antique silver. When she was told that there were those who tried to discredit her story, she was deeply upset. Anna said that her father may have put the skull up for sale, as he often did with other pieces in his collection in order to raise money, and then after some years, may have bought it back. If this were the case, then Anna's story still holds.

Perhaps Mitchell-Hedges felt he had to auction and buy back the skull for political and/or other reasons of which we are not aware. We will never know the answer to these mysteries, so it is up to you, the reader, to decide what is fact or fiction.

The year was 1924 and Anna, a sixteen-year-old girl, had accompanied her father on an expedition to Belize, then known as British Honduras. F.A. Mitchell-Hedges is said to have loved a good adventure and through the years travelled the world in search of ancient civilizations. It is said that the movie character Indiana Jones was partly based on Mitchell-Hedges' real life adventures. An avid explorer, his desire on this particular journey was to find the remains of the lost continent of Atlantis, which at the time he believed to be in the area around the Cayman Islands, off the coast of Belize. Anna and her father had spent a lot of time with the Maya and they were now in a tiny place called Lubantuun.

Anna told me that it had been a hot day and her father and those that were with them on the expedition were having a siesta. But Anna wasn't tired and the heat hadn't bothered her. She wanted to look at where they were and so climbed on top of some stone ruins and took in the view. As she looked down, she saw something sparkling on the ground far below. Excited, she called to her father and told him that she had seen something shiny. He scolded her for having left the campsite as it could have been dangerous but she must have been very persuasive as the next day they started clearing a path through the jungle to get to the ruins.

On her seventeenth birthday, Anna found the skull. She was lowered down into the ruin and without knowing what it was that she had found, picked up the top half of the skull. She pressed the object closely to her chest and tugged on the rope that supported her to be lifted back up to where the others were waiting. Back on firm ground, she proudly presented her find to her father. The Maya gathered in awe at what had been found. Her father soon realized that this was no ordinary object and one that was in fact highly revered. He gave this sacred object to the Mayan High Priest. The celebration lasted for days and people came from all around to join in the festivities. The crystal skull had been found!

Anna and her father stayed for three years and when it was time to return home, the High Priest handed a bundle to Mitchell-Hedges, saying that the skull would be better off if they took it with them – that it would be in safe hands. And so Anna, her father, and the ancient crystal skull travelled back to England – a journey and a destiny that has shaped what was to come.

ABOUT THE AUTHOR

Solange Arbesú–Sala was born in Cuba and grew up in Montreal, Canada. In the early 1990's Solange attended a lecture in Santa Cruz, California about the mystery surrounding the crystal skulls. The result was a profound change in the perception of her personal relationship to the world. She describes it as an awakening, a connection to an inner knowledge of which she was previously unaware. What followed was more than 20 years of study of ancient, esoteric wisdom with spiritual teachers from many traditions. *Ancient Memories Future Dreams, the Crystal Skull Diaries* is her debut novel.

Solange is also a certified Human Design Analyst and has built a reputation for readings that integrate intuition with compassion, clarity, and practical wisdom. She lives in San Francisco.

For more information please visit:
www.solangearbesu-sala.com

www.ingramcontent.com/pod-product-compliance
Lightning Source LLC
Chambersburg PA
CBHW030648110726
47901CB00002B/618